Breaking and Entering

ILLINOIS SHORT FICTION

BREAKING AND ENTERING

Stories by Peter Makuck

UNIVERSITY OF ILLINOIS PRESS

Urbana   Chicago   London

Publication of this work was supported in part by a grant from the Illinois Art Council, a state agency.

"Assumption," *The Sewanee Review,* 83 (Winter 1975).
"The Enemy," *Mississippi Review,* 5 (Summer 1976).
"In a Field of Force," *The Virginia Quarterly Review,* 50 (Fall 1974).
"How It Fee-yuls," *The Carleton Miscellany,* 26 (Fall-Winter 1976-77).
"Breaking and Entering," *The Sewanee Review,* 88 (Summer 1980).
"Big in Osaka," *The Virginia Quarterly Review,* 56 (Summer 1980).
"Don't Call Us, We'll Call You," originally published as "Secret," *The Southern Review,* 15 (Spring 1979).
"Paper Options," *The Greensboro Review,* 25 (Winter 1978-79).

Library of Congress Cataloging in Publication Data

Makuck, Peter, 1940–
   Breaking and entering.

   (Illinois short fiction)
   Contents: Assumption — The enemy — In a field
of force — [etc.]
   I. Title. II. Series.
PS3563.A396B7   813'.54   81-3406
ISBN 0-252-00898-7 (cloth)   AACR2
ISBN 0-252-00925-8 (paper)

For Phyllis

Poor intricated soul! Riddling, perplexed,
labyrinthical soul!

John Donne

Contents

Assumption

His father said, "Of course he wants to go."

His mother said, "But last time he was late and Sister telephoned about his dungarees."

"Don't worry, we'll get home in time to change, won't we?"

Danny looked at his mom, whose eyes softened from their hard metal grayness. She smiled. Mom was always worried about the sisters and priests. She even drove the sisters here and there because, poor things, they had nobody to help them and it was just awful. But Mom smiled and Danny was glad.

"Better hit the sack," said Dad and he held out his arms, cocked, as he did every night. Danny gripped the big wrists. "Ready?" asked Dad. Danny looked from his father's face to the powerful chest, the plot of hair that pressed darkly against the white undershirt. Dad had just come home, and there was a smell of trees and beer. Dad's arms and shoulders were veiny and muscled like the pictures of Greek statues in his history book. He watched the muscles stand and gleam as he felt his own feet leave the floor. Slowly, with great effort, Danny pulled himself five times to the level of his father's shivering cheek dotted with stubble. Then his feet touched the floor. "Atta boy!" said Dad, mussing his hair and sending him upstairs with a pat on the butt. Mom smiled in a funny way. Dad said, "I wanna hear those bed springs in two minutes."

"Yes," said Mom, "after he says his prayers."

The window next to his bed was tall, and the glass was streaked with silver because the shade was up and there was a moon. Danny stretched under the sheets that were clean and cool. Squint and the moon sent long needles of light to your eyes. Heaven was beyond the farthest star—that was what Sister Paulita said. Sister had a red face that quivered and a glass eye that goggled, but you couldn't hate her because that was a sin. Danny didn't want to commit sins because that made you die. If you were good, very good, you might not have to die; you might get to heaven alive, like some of the saints. In heaven there were beautiful trees, said Sister, more beautiful than anything on earth, with fruit so delicious it was impossible to describe. Larry, the boy in the next seat, asked if you could remember earth from heaven.

"Yes," said Sister.

The room was very still. Ominously the clock hand jumped with a loud tick toward ten: arithmetic. Then Larry asked how there could be perfect happiness if you looked around and didn't see your brothers and sisters or parents. Sister said they could be in purgatory. But what if year after year they didn't get to heaven? Sister said there was no time in heaven and if your parents or brothers and sisters were really in hell, God would give you amnesia.

"Magnesia?"

"*Am*nesia is a sickness that makes you forget."

Again it was very quiet. Larry swiveled his eyes from Mike to Danny. A faint grin came to his lips. "But how can you be perfectly happy if you're sick with magnesia." Someone made a noise like breaking wind. A cough. Several giggles. Students bowed their heads and reddened with held-in laughter. Danny's stomach tightened with fear. Sister's face went funny, quivered, and got the color of boiled ham. The glass eye goggled and bulged toward Danny as Sister said to Larry, "Master Eduardo, you can see me after school." Danny stiffened. After school meant missing the bus and home was far—how would you get there? She picked up a piece of chalk and drew a box at the upper end of the blackboard. The chalk broke to bits and splashed on the warped wooden floor. Sister angrily groped for another stick and scribbled Larry's name in the box, where it would remain all day. "Anyone else?" she wheezed, her red stare raking the class. "Very well then," she said, adjusting her black veil and white bib, "take out your arithmetic books and open to page fifty-four."

But Danny didn't have to open his book because it was black, then half-dark, and his father's face hung over the bed like a big pale moon. "Come on," he whispered, "get dressed and I'll be back with the truck in ten minutes or so."

Danny sat on the wooden stairs and laced his sneakers. The stars were single and in clusters like the jacks that girls threw at recess; they sparkled and pricked your eyes. The neighborhood world seemed huge and deep and lonely. The trees loomed and stood nearby like guardian angels. Crickets and tree frogs cheeped. God made everything and not even a grain of sand could exist without Him. The white truck rattled around the corner, and Danny jumped into the open door while it still coasted. Movies. Cowboys leaping from the saddle to moving trains.

Dad's face was lit from below by the panel: he had cheeks and a nose but no eyes. "Now we'll get a bite," he shouted over the clanking of bottles and for several miles they clinked and clanked through the deserted dark, through STOP signs and flashing red traffic lights. "What if a cop . . . ?" yelled Danny. Dad turned his head and smiled and said, "Cops don't care about milk trucks, not at this time of day." They slowed at the end of the bridge, and a black woman with a gold tooth leaned out of the toll booth and took the orange ticket.

The diner was crowded with men and smells. "Hey, Tom, down here," came a loud voice from the end of the counter. Danny recognized another driver named Larkin, whose face was scarred and looked like a puzzle because of an accident with the truck and all the broken bottles that fell on him. Danny climbed up on the stool and, like the men, tried to hook his heels into the bottom rung, but they wouldn't reach so he let them dangle. Dad hunched over the counter and talked. Danny listened to the jukebox songs and watched different men in the mirror. Dressed in a brown ratty coat with grease stains was an old man with red eyes and wrinkled gray skin; he kept working at his nose with a dirty handkerchief at the same time he ate a muffin. Deep in the mirror, in one of the booths, were a sailor and a woman with yellow hair. The sailor had red stripes on his black sleeve, and he sat with his arm around the woman and stared into her face. Their heads were close together. Once in a while they kissed. They seemed all by themselves, even though the diner was very crowded and noisy.

"Whattya gonna have?" asked the waitress. She looked as old as Danny's mom, but she was different. Her dress was up high, and it was so tight her chest stuck out. And her lips were curvy and red as the catsup on Larkin's plate. The men all laughed because Larkin said, "What he wants ain't on the menu."

"I didn't say that," Dad said, holding up his hands in defense.

"I know," said the waitress, "that shithead did. Now come on, I gotta hustle."

And Mom would never use words like that. Waiting for his scrambled eggs and bacon, Danny's looks went from the sailor to the man with the dirty handkerchief to the waitress who hustled up and down behind the counter with a cigarette dangling from her lips. Smoking in public was cheap, said Mom, and smoking, period, was a sign of weakness. Danny looked at the distant floor between his legs: gum wrappers, cellophane, cigarette butts with a black smear of ash and the brown weedy guts. Danny looked up. The old man finally put away his dirty handkerchief and revealed his big club nose that was peppered with blackheads. Larkin's face, a patchwork of red and purple, twisted as he asked: "And you think you can get away with that?"

"Shit, yes," said Dad.

Danny shuddered, put his hand on his father's leg, lifted his eyes imploringly. "Whattya want?" asked Dad. Danny couldn't say; he tried to smile and look away. The old man was at his nose again.

The waitress roughly clacked down their plates. "What's ta drink?" she coughed.

Danny said, "Milk."

Dad said, "Coffee, black."

In the big white lake of the plate, the eggs seemed small; the bacon too. The yellow eggs leaked a clear oil, and the bacon was limp and fatty and cold. Danny's hunger shrank. He put some catsup on the plate but that didn't help at all, and he choked down several forkfuls before quitting. Suddenly he wanted to be out in the night world again.

A hand ruffled Danny's hair and a voice asked: "Who's this guy?" It was Seymour, and he sat on the next red stool.

"Hey, what's up?" asked Dad.

"Got help this morning, I see." Seymour wore the white uniform and cap. The uniform had different colored stains: ink, chocolate, orange. The other drivers wore uniforms but not Dad because it was stupid, fruity. Seymour said, "So tell me, Dan, how ya doin'?"

Danny smiled and said, "Good." He liked Seymour. Seymour paid attention to you and was funny and knew lots of riddles. "Man, lookit all that hair! Wish I had some of it." Seymour took off his cap and smoothed back one of two hairs left on his shiny skull. Larkin laughed and said that Seymour didn't have any hair because he didn't get enough. Danny asked Dad how you could get some if you didn't have any. Maybe it was a riddle.

"How do you get it?" asked Larkin. "Easy!"

And they all laughed again.

Seymour waved them away with his hand. The sailor and the woman with yellow hair went out the door. Another sailor came in; he staggered and slumped into an empty booth. In a few minutes, the waitress went to his table to take his order, but the sailor was asleep. She shook him by the shoulder, but he wouldn't wake up.

"You gave it to ol' Miller," said Seymour.

"Yeah," said Dad, grinning.

"But he's probably talkin' to the boss right now."

"Shit, let um." Danny winced. He didn't like to hear his dad use those words. They were sins; they made black specks on your soul. God would punish you.

"Say, what route you on today?"

"Six, like always. Why?"

"Listen, when you're finished—"

"Yeah, I know—swing by and pick up the kid."

Dad smiled, explained: "The kid got in dutch with the nun. Besides, I got collections today."

Seymour hiked his cheek and shook his head. "Yeah, collections."

They went around the big traffic oval: Mr. Donut . . .
Sunoco . . . Delac Chevy . . . State Police. . . . But instead
of the usual way through town, Dad went off the oval and followed
the river road that would take them under the bridge. The truck
lights bounced and lanced through the darkness and banks of
white mist. "Take a half pint of milk and open a package of
donuts—you didn't eat nothin' back there. Don't want your mother
squawkin', now do we?"

"Can I have chocolate?"

"Yeah, go ahead."

Danny opened a half pint of chocolate and bit into a cinnamon
donut. The road was bumpy, and sometimes the bottle clicked
against his teeth. It was hard to keep his balance. The panel lights
sharpened Dad's nose and cheeks. He was tall and hunched over the
wheel as he drove standing up, squinting into the misty dark, the
eyes still hidden.

"Where are we going?" asked Danny.

"Route number nine. You never been on this one, have you? I
didn't think so. This is Collinson's route." Dad laughed. "Fast
work." He turned his face and smiled and gave Danny a zip on the
top of the head. "We'll have some fun, right?"

Danny said, "Right." Dad could make you laugh. All the other
drivers liked him, laughed with him. If only he didn't say bad
words. Sister said you should pray for your parents because God
loves to hear the voices of little children, listens more carefully to
children because their souls are still pure. Sometimes when Dad said
bad words it was funny, but Danny knew he shouldn't laugh.

Under the bridge the concrete footings stood away in the dark like
huge white crosses. Danny watched the road and saw the red furry
remains of some small animal. He felt bad. Did animals have souls?
He wondered. "Ready, Dan? First stop coming up." They slowed,
stopped before a lonely little bungalow with a white picket fence.
Dad pulled up the clicking handbrake. "Two homo," he said. His
hands were big, the fingers like thick twists of cowboy rope, brown.
With one hand, he lifted two white bottles. "Here you go, side

porch, be careful.'' Danny took one bottle in each hand and jumped into the dark.

He went through the creaky gate and found the metal box at the foot of the porch stairs. One then the other, he set the bottles in with a glassy clink and drew out the empties that smelled faintly sour. He stuck his fingers in the necks and carried both bottles one-handed. Sometimes, when he didn't want to fool with the carrier, Dad would take three in each hand. Three! And full! Danny sprang into the truck and Dad said, ''Atta boy! Now we're cookin' with gas.''

The stops were getting closer. The river was still on the left, and the smell of salt was thick and constant and when they stopped he could hear the foghorn go *ooo* in the distance. Streetlamps hung like moons in the mist. ''Now we're coming to the project,'' said Dad, ''and we'll smoke up this load in no time.'' The big white sign read CONNING TOWERS HOUSING. At the entrance arch there was a real conning tower with a set of deck guns on either side. Dad said, ''If we've got time later, you can set up behind one of them ack-acks.''

They went up and down streets, and the houses looked pretty much the same. Danny had the feeling they were going in circles There were no trees. Different cars were the only landmarks. Dad shouted orders, and Danny jumped off the truck while it was still rolling. It made him feel big. Dad said, ''Beat ya back,'' but Danny almost always made it first. Then he stood on the running board and listened for the sound of change jingling in Dad's pocket. Sometimes he had to wait a long time while Dad collected. The foghorn went *ooo*, and dogs prowled around the truck.

Dad shifted into gear. They went up the street and turned the corner. ''Over there, around the back,'' said Dad. ''Two skim. I'll pick you up here on the way back.'' The ruby taillights faded into the dark, and the gears whined away. It was quiet again, and Danny made his way around the house past two big silver cylinders that looked like bombs. He climbed the long flight of stairs, left the milk, and had one foot on the sidewalk when a woman in a shiny black kimono stepped onto the porch. The kimono was like a bed quilt, and it had a snow-capped mountain on it. Danny stood at the bottom of the stairs and looked up. The woman had long silky hair.

She stooped for the milk and took a bottle in each hand. The kimono opened, and Danny saw a wedge of black curly hair where the white legs met. He felt he should hide or not move and hoped she would not see him. But she did and said, "Ahh!" Then she smiled and clutched the kimono to herself. Danny stepped into the plank of light sent by the opened door and told her his name. She smiled in a curious way. "Well," she said, "tell your daddy Mrs. Davis says she'll be here all morning if he wants to collect."

Danny lugged the carrier and clinking bottles to the porch of the next house. He lifted the box lid and put in the cold white bottle. The lip flapped, and he jumped from the stairs. He still saw the black wedge. It was so strange. Maybe he shouldn't think of it. There was a growl at his back. He turned. A small dog with a black coat was inching toward him with its nose curled and teeth showing whitely in the dark. Stick your carrier at um, said Dad, and don't show um you're scared. But he was. Now it began to dance and bark in circles around him. Teeth coming and going in the dark. Snaps. Grrrr. Then the dog ran away. It was very still. The foghorn went *ooo,* and Danny heard the growing sound of the truck grinding, the bottles clanking.

Dad figured in the book.

The truck vibrated.

"Dad?"

"What?"

"I can't be late to school because Sister ———"

Dad turned. "Hey, it's still dark." He made a funny face. "You know what?"

"What?"

"We'll tell Sister to go piss up a rope."

Danny laughed. Then he knew he shouldn't have.

"And I'll punch Father What's-his-name a good one."

Danny frowned.

"Okay, okay, don't worry, Seymour'll be by to take you." Dad filled the carrier and told Danny what to leave where. "Wait for me over there," he said. "Remember, don't leave nothin' at the last house."

Danny lugged the heavy carrier. There was a ticking, humming noise coming from the cylinders at the sides of houses. Piss was a bad word. He shouldn't have laughed. And to hit a priest was a mortal sin. Dear God, please help Daddy. Sister Paulita held up a sheet of paper, clean and white. She began making dots with a pencil. "Each sin darkens your soul," she said. "Mortal sins do this." She made a round black spot the size of a silver dollar. "But as Catholics," she said, "we are lucky, lucky because we have confession which"—she began to erase—"cleanses the soul and cuts down, but not completely, the temporal punishment due to sin, the time you spend in purgatory."

At the corner he put down the carrier of empties and waited. Under the streetlamp he could see that one of the bottles had soggy cigarettes in it, some with pink lipstick marks. They were filthy and made him shudder. It was quiet and nothing moved. There was no sound from the truck. Minutes passed. He thought about the woman in the black kimono. Then there was a *grrr* behind him. The dog again. He grabbed the carrier and tried to think of St. Francis, but the dog crept closer. Then there was a great thunderclap, and the dog ran away. Danny wondered if it would rain. Then he noticed the red glow above the rooftops, the sparks and gray smoke against the darker sky. Only a few blocks away. Maybe Dad would take time, and they would go to see what it was. But he didn't come, and Danny, before he knew why, was running. He came to a wire fence, climbed it, and, at the top, fell. The world looped, flashed, and came back. A sapling maple seemed to topple toward him until he was on his feet again.

One house had no front and only part of a roof that flames lapped and leaped above. The great body of fire leaned until the next house smoked. People were running, some with bare legs. The fire crackled loudly and began to roar. Shouts came from all directions. Where was Dad? The truck was at the corner, but when he got to it, empty. His heart fell. A few boys and girls and their mothers huddled in groups across the street, away from the heat. He searched for his father among the faces. He stopped a barefooted man in jeans: "I can't find my father. He's a milkman." But the man snarled:

"Git back outta here," pointed across the street, and ran off. Now the wind was bigger, and the flames leaned more. The lawn was full of smoky debris. A mattress lay twisted and humped in the street. A man in white underwear ran from the door of a house that was beginning to go. Coughing doubled him over. He backed away. Voices rose, thin, desperate, full of unbelief. A woman ran to him, her chest bouncing; she wore a pink house dress, and her legs came out of the slit. A red glare brightened somewhere deep in the house and dimly lighted the windows. Danny saw a figure within the glare framed by a window. It was his father! Cradling something like a football, he stopped in the doorway then plunged through the smoke, coughing like the other man who now ran forward and took a small child.

"Dad, Dad!"

"Get back, back," yelled his father. There was a loud crack, and a veil of orange sparks rose in the sky. Dad was yelling, coughing. His eyes and mouth were round black holes in the flickering light. His lip curled away from the teeth almost in anger. "Dammit, get back." And he gave Danny a shove. The man was screaming too: "Upstairs." And a man in blue pajamas yelled, "Firemen . . . wait."

But his father turned to the house. "Don't," cried Danny; "Dad!" He grabbed at him, but his hand was left outstretched toward the shrinking form, and as Danny watched him jump through the black rectangle of a doorway, the roof dissolved into flames. There was a gust of heat. Danny, next to the man in pajamas, backed away, tripped. It was a cat, on its side, dead, stinking in its burned fur. Someone strongly gripped his arms and lifted—it was Seymour. Danny realized that for some moments now a siren had been howling in the orange leaping air. Firemen shouted to each other in long black coats with white letters on the back and jumped on and off the loud red engines. Shiny hoses, thick, snaked on the lawn, then stiffened with water, and a noise went up from the house. "Come on, Danny." But Danny fought and cried, fought long enough to see, as if cut from black construction paper, his father's shape in the window, with something sacked over his shoulder, flames clinging to his back and arms and legs, as he burst through the burning wall and the sack—now a woman—rolled in flames, and firemen fell upon them both. White figures from one of the ambulances rolled a cot, and Seymour carried Danny to his truck. "Your Dad's going to be OK," Seymour said over and over. "The doctors will give him complete attention, Danny. He'll be OK, try not to worry."

Then it was dawn and Seymour's truck nosed along the river toward the bridge, and red sunlight was bleeding into the sky from behind the trees, and the world went backward and away.

That afternoon, Danny looked closely at his mother's watery, gray eyes and asked: "If you was God, you would let him live, wouldn't you?"

His mother smoothed his hair and gazed emptily at the yellow sun moving on the bare floor. "Yes, yes, of course," she said, coming back.

"I would too," said Danny. Clocktick deepened the quiet, and everything was tense and afraid. Danny walked from room to room, touching familiar objects now odd, queer. He wondered what he had done since Seymour had left, but there were only moments, like rooms, and when you were in one, you could not know what was in the other.

Then, in the kitchen, after the call came, and the phone clung silently, blackly to the wallpaper roses, his mother sagged onto one of the creaky wooden chairs at the table. She made him come to her. "Your father," she said; her voice was small, scratchy, and her shoulders trembled. For a moment she did not go on but held him tightly, so tightly that it almost hurt his arms. Her body smelled of dry sweat covered with lilacs that were too sweet. And when she spoke, her breath was sour. "Your father, Danny"—this time she held him with arms straight and talked as though a tear had not snagged on her rimless spectacles, dropped to her pale bloodless cheek where it met another shiny trickle, and slid down through the many branching lines that he had never seen before—"Daddy is not going to get better." She studied his face. "He won't come home anymore, never, ever." Danny's breath came hard. "Do you understand?"

Danny began to shake. "Why?" he cried.

"Because God loved him and took him because he was in so much pain."

"But you said God could let him live."

"Danny," she pleaded, "we must not question God. He sends suffering to those he loves most."

"Why?"

"Someday you'll understand."

"He's dead!"

She shook her head no, bit her lip. "He's in heaven." She was crying freely now. Danny could not breathe. I'll never see him again, ever. *Never, ever.* The words repeated themselves again and again. Playing catch, laughing, the smell of his hair, the steel of his arms—*never, ever.* The words created a dark lake from which his father rescued him in bad dreams. Now never. Who would save him? His chest broke into great spasms, like retching, and wild hot rivers ran down his cheeks, and the world was blurred and salt burned on his panting lips.

The house was two away from the convent; it was big and of white clapboard and over the porch was a blue awning that said in white letters: DOLAND FUNERAL HOME. Sister Paulita brought his classmates. They filed past slowly, quietly on the heavy carpets, and their passing bodies made the air jostle and brought to Danny waves of flower smell that were too sweet. His Uncle Joe stood behind with a hand occasionally on Danny's shoulder. Father Altier, the principal, sprinkled holy water on the grainy lid, and the silver drops stood, then slid like tears. Danny firmed himself—Dad would want it. "Requiem aeternam dona ei, Domine," prayed Father, and Danny listened to the mysterious powerful words that would cleanse his father's soul. "Exsultabunt Domino ossa humiliata. . . ." Sister's grave, starched-in face looked at Danny, stared the way it did when you were bad, but why? Danny looked away, looked furtively at the faces of his classmates for some recognition. Sister had ranged and tiered them on the other side of the casket, faraway and floating against the deep folds of the darkly curtained wall. None seemed to see him. He wondered if Billy, Jack, or Dickie was sorry. Or any of the others. Sister blew a "C" from her little silver pipe.

Danny watched the singing faces, dark holes appearing and disappearing at the same time. Sister's hands directed; they swooped and flickered like white bats. "Kyrie, eleison. Christe, eleison." The same words, over and over, stretched out, held, tortured and lovely. God would listen. In the car his uncle looked at him. "Danny," he said. Danny looked at the flesh above the fresh white collar; it had teeny pimples and made a little loaf that squeezed the neck when the chin was back, moving: "Danny, you're a brave little man."

In this section there were lots of trees, the branches of some still bare; others were evergreen. The morning was sunny, a bit cold, empty, and quiet. They parked the cars in a line, and everyone got out. Seymour and some of the other drivers slowly, very carefully, carried the casket to the grave, then everyone else came forward. Uncle Joe broke a bouquet of yellow flowers on the wooden lid and, long-stemmed, they lay like tangled pickup sticks. Wind snapped at the green tent and hummed on the taut ropes. Father Altier prayed again: "Oremus . . . In paradisium deducant te Angeli. . . . " His aunts dangled rosary beads and from time to time sniffled and lifted their black veils to dab their eyes with Kleenex. They stared down at the casket, frowning, very slightly shaking their heads. Daddy was inside, part of him. Here and not here. His soul had black specks like the ones that were on his cheek at night. But he saved some people from the flames—the newspaper said so. Dear Jesus, please save my daddy from the flames. "Ego sum resurrectio et vita. . . . " The trees swayed like angels. Flames stuck to his back and legs and arms as he ran from the house. He would leave purgatory that way too and live forever with God, and Danny would see him again. Father Altier sprinkled the wooden lid. Now he prayed in English: "The days of man are short. . . . " Danny stared at all the bitter gray and white stones and the small burial houses of marble. " . . . Unto judgment with Thee . . . clean that is conceived of unclean seed. . . . " Slowly the coffin began to descend. Under the fake grass Danny saw a patch, then a whole slab of brown raw earth. "Remember, man, that thou art dust. . . . "

Here and not here. Gone. Dead. No, not that.

In bed, Danny gazed at the diamond stars in his tall window. Daddy was not in hell; he had received extreme unction from Father Altier; he was in heaven or purgatory, out in the stars, or beyond. Danny did not want to sleep, dream of the dark lake. Last night he did not dream, nor before that. If only he could go to God without dying. Some saints had been permitted, because they were pure. Sister Paulita said that purification comes from sacrifice, from doing what we don't want to because the flesh is weak. So Danny had begun, on the first day, to empty the trash and wet garbage, to force himself to wash out the terrible coffee grounds. He swept the porch and shoveled ash from the furnace. Then there was nothing to do, nothing to look forward to. He said rosaries, one after another, but had no idea how many it would take if he were in purgatory. He walked through the back field to the sand pit. There was nothing to do, nothing to look forward to. The sun was low and red and caught in the trees. Frogs croaked, but Danny did not feel like catching them, didn't feel like skipping stones on the green, clear water. Dad would no longer come out here with him. The fields, woods, sand pit were not the same. Nothing was like nothing any more. *Never, ever.* And he cried and cried.

Today he rode to school in the milk truck because Mom had to take care of something with a lawyer. Seymour gave him riddles and made jokes, and Danny laughed to be polite. He thanked Seymour and watched the truck rattle away. In the side windows of the cathedral Danny saw the saints who looked sadly down from their stained, puzzlelike windows. Sister said that almost no one went straight to heaven and that's why you should pray for the souls in purgatory. Some day you'll need prayers yourself. Danny slowly took the cement stairway down to the playground. The black pipe railings were silver on the top from where the boys sat and balanced and slid. The cathedral threw a veil of shadow over the brick school. Dear Jesus, please help my dad, please make me pure. Some girls were sitting on the steps of the girls' section; they were throwing silver jacks and snatching them up between bounces of the small red ball. The sky was low and blank, and the sun ghosted in and out of the white mist. The foghorn went *ooo* in the harbor, and the world was half-hidden.

Jim and Dickie closed in on him as he reached the playground. Dickie was big and had a belly and a long neck and a little head like Danny's pet turtle. Jim looked like a frog and had frizzy blond hair. They looked at each other and grinned.

"You think you're big stuff," said Jim.

"Yah, a goody-goody," said Dickie.

"Just to get in good with Sista," said another and made kiss-kiss noises. They all laughed.

"No sir!"

"Yes sir, just because your ol' man died."

Danny shook his head.

One of the others said: "My ol' man said that milkmen"—he waited for everyone to listen—"milkmen get a lot of nookie."

They laughed, and then Jim said, "Ah, lookit um, let's get outta here, he's just a baby."

Danny scuffed toward the tree by the wire fence and stayed out after the bell. The yard was terribly empty. The foghorn went *ooo,* and in a light breeze a newspaper descended with spread wings and crashed into the corner of the church. Then it rolled around the corner, and Danny followed it to where Sister could not see from the classroom. He leaned against cold stone. His name would now go into the chalk square on the blackboard. Sister might tug him to the front of the class like Larry and call him a goofus. Only once had he been to the dark cloakroom: the smell of wet wool mittens and light leaking around the edges of the door like hope. What had he done? Judy, the monitor, said he had spoken when Sister was out of the room. He stood in the cold dark, and then the door, after several hours, burst open, and he squinted. Sister stood with hands on her wide hips. She said, "So you haven't learned your lesson, I see," and shut the door again. Danny could see his name in the chalk square. He wanted to go home, but home was so far and bus tickets were no good now and Mom would be mad. If only Dad . . . Seymour—maybe he could walk to the dairy.

He hurried past Harry's candy store toward the A & P. Sister might send a boy to look. He had better get away. The foghorn went *ooo,* and he thought of the woman with the black kimono, the mountain. Jesus prayed on top of a mountain. He cut through the alley by the Jew store and went up the street. Now there was a haze over the sun, and it looked like a white communion host. He saw the faces of Jim and Dickie, but knew that he must not hate because they did not know what they were doing. To hate was a sin; it made you die. Dear Jesus, please help me. I want to see my father and not die.

As he dug into the hill by the jail, the gold cross of the cathedral steeple followed him and stood between and over buildings until he reached the old Lyceum theater. The boarded entrance was covered with faded circus posters and scribbled names and carved hearts. It was here that he sometimes waited for the bus. A woman in a tan raincoat went past him carrying a big shopping bag with a red A & P; she looked at him strangely. He was in the wrong place. He did not belong to this part of the nine o'clock world. Better get off the street. But where? A dirty white pigeon wheeled down; it fanned its tail feathers to break speed, snatched something from the gutter, and made a loud flapping climb, at last disappearing over the roof. Then Danny knew. He waited until the coast was clear and slipped off the street.

A sharp unpleasant smell seeped up from the damp stone in the narrow alley behind the theater. Danny had only heard the stories, but now he looked up and saw the window with the boards ripped off. One of the older boys told how to do it: you put your back to one wall and walk your feet up the other. Danny tried it and easily reached the window. Then one hand at a time on the sill and jump down. It was a small room with a dressing table and an overturned chair. The mirror was cracked and most of the lights around it were broken. Glass crackled under his shoes as he walked to the open door and into the dim corridor. There was light at the end, and Danny groped his way toward it, climbed two stairs, and walked more confidently onto the stage. His footsteps echoed loudly, the way they did in an empty church. Dust-dotted slats of leaden light tilted into the darkness from the boarded windows and holes in the roof. Pigeons exploded in the rafters. Danny looked up and saw one of the birds momentarily darken a hole. He walked on creaking

boards to the apron of the stage and climbed into the orchestra pit.
Older boys had said there were rats. Dear St. Francis, please help
me. If it would happen, the best place would be somewhere high,
like in the holy picture over Mom's bed: the Blessed Mother, a
cloud, a mountain, and the town below.

He made his way haltingly up the main aisle, stopping now and
then to listen. The carpet had holes and wine-colored figures. Seats
were whitened with pigeon droppings. Yellow stuffing and gobs of
cotton grew from the torn covering. Draped on the back of a seat
was a shriveled white balloon, long and narrow. Danny walked
carefully because the other boys said the floors were weak and you
could fall into the basement where the rats were. But the floor was
solid. A white feather twirled through the light and balanced on one
of the seatbacks. But now, by the refreshment counter, it was much
darker. At either side of the main door were two yellow metal urns
that dimly glowed.

Danny took the stairs to the second balcony. Cooing of the birds
was louder. He paused and looked into the dark space crisscrossed
with beams of light; one came near him and touched the wall of the
next stairwell. Someone had scratched *Nigger Heaven* deeply into
the plaster, and there was an arrow pointing up. Danny turned and
climbed. He emerged in the third balcony. It was small and circular.
The stage below seemed very small, almost straight down. He went
up the aisle of wooden seats toward the booth, toward the ladder
that went to a trap door. There was a square of yellow light
overhead, and Danny scrambled through.

He squinted. The gold cross of the steeple was still above him and
not far away, but the city was now at his feet. He breathed deeply to
get his wind. It was the right place, and he was glad he had come. He
hoped he had not already become too old with sin. A siren wailed
and grew louder and lost itself in the maze below. Dear Jesus, he
whispered. Between the roof peaks, he could see the lonely, empty
school yard. He walked to the edge. Tiny people got on the bus,
which roared away leaving a black cloud behind. A foghorn
groaned in the harbor. He faced the cross; it flashed like a knife
blade. He backed well away from the edge. In the middle of the
roof, high up, God could easily see him. Sister said to please kneel,

close your eyes, and pray for the souls in purgatory. He closed his eyes tightly to get the holy darkness for prayer. Sharp pebbles cut into his knees. Again the foghorn groaned, and Danny prayed to the holy intimate dark behind his eyelids. Dear Jesus, I want to see my father. . . . But he had barely begun when the wood beneath his knees exploded, and he felt a rush of wind and black sinking, as in sleep just before he would cry out and wake to his father's face and the strong surrounding arms.

The Enemy

At the farm he would sit on the porch swing and listen to the wood groan and watch the hawks riding thermals, hanging, teetering, slowly turning the sky, exploding, and reappearing out of the August sun. And more than once he saw one buckle its wings, plummet, then heavily beat its way upward with a hen or dangling rabbit. And once he saw his grandfather burst from the barn, lead one with a shotgun, and blast it from the late afternoon sky, feathers and fluff slowly parachuting into the pasture beyond the barbed wire. But it was the picture of them riding the thermals and slowly turning that stayed in David's mind.

In fifth grade, he drew planes in his spiral notebook and, at the risk of being caught by Sister Scholastica, flew dime gliders from the fourth level of the green firestairs where, before launch, he would breathe on the wings and stabilizer, warping the surfaces for longer flight.

Later came the more sophisticated gliders with dihedral wings and substantial airfoils that you made from kits; these he would launch in the as-yet unplanted part of the cemetery near home and run below when they caught an updraft and stayed aloft for a minute or more, coming down for miraculous landings between the perilous upright stones. Sometimes, though, they were smashed to pieces. But that was all right: not *all* the fun was in the flying, and David spent wonderful nights in his cellar, hunched over his workbench, razoring splendid white sheets of balsa into ribs, struts, spars, and fuselage sections. He inhabited a timeless world of glue, transistor rock, and the transporting fumes of Aerogloss lacquer. David's desire to beat gravity was insatiable; the planes grew larger, more intricate. One had wings that folded back and was flung fifty to sixty feet into the air by slingshot, so that the wings, at the top of trajectory, would pop out, and the glider float in slow, circling descent. And there were the prop-driven planes with great wingspans that climbed to a height of 200 feet on a rubber-band engine. Beautifully drifting, these would stay aloft three or four minutes, sometimes longer. Once he lost such a plane; it got caught in a thermal and soared, freely and far, becoming a small red dot and disappearing, painfully, as he pedaled vainly after it on his bike.

Then, inevitably, came the gas engine, a Christmas gift. He began building planes that were controlled from the ground on long wires fixed to a handle. They weren't as free, as neat, as simple, as beautiful, but they were more real, took off from the ground, and maneuvered like real aircraft. Now when he went out to fly, he lugged a toolbox in which he kept the heavy dry cell battery, the green pint can of Powermist fuel with the picture of a biplane and checkered flag, black plastic U-Reely handle, wooden Topflight props, glue, gaskets, silk patches, and glow plugs. After school, in the late afternoons, his first gas-powered aircraft, a navy blue Avenger, droned like a chainsaw, as it dove and looped above the white stones.

Gliding and free flight were over.

Before David knew it, his father was prodding him to join a model club that the son of one of his business friends belonged to. It was a way to meet others, said Dad, enter competition, learn new building techniques. Reluctantly, David gave up solitary building and flying. Now, on weekends, he was going to Lantern Hill Farms where the club, the Aero Prop-Busters, rented a great open field for practice meetings. Mike, the club president, a man of thirty whose face bore a purple stringlike scar from ear to chin, told the boys various ways to prepare for the summer contests. "You should have a first event," said Mike, "plus a few others, 'cause on total points, we're shootin' for club trophies too. Listen, when you walk onto that field wearing a Prop-Buster shirt, you want them other guys to *tremble,* right?''

The boys said, "Right.''

"What?''

"RIGHT!''

David's event was Stunt. Judges rated you from one to ten on each step of your performance of the AMA flight pattern: level upright and inverted flight, inside and outside loops, eights (overhead, vertical, horizontal, square, triangular), takeoff, and landing. David loved Stunt for its order, beauty, grace. Besides, it was something you did alone.

His second event was Combat: two extremely fast, maneuverable aircraft, on lines of equal length, chased each other through loops, dives, and other evasive and stalking actions in an attempt to clip off the ten-foot crepe-paper streamer towed by each. Bodies bumped, U-Reelys clacked together, and there were often crashes. Even though the Combat ship wasn't beautiful or special, you still didn't like to see it explode to bits in a crash. Sometimes, in a missed pass, the aircraft would collide, lock together in an embrace of death, and spiral in—both equally demolished. Then it was easy to laugh. No hard feelings. David, on those greening afternoons at Lantern Hill Farms, quickly got good, even at Combat. A number of times, he had beaten the club's best, Avery, a guy who was twenty-two. Still, though, Stunt was his favorite. The aircraft was such a neat thing, it wasn't right, somehow, to make it fight, crash to pieces.

The day before his first contest, after he had made repairs and last minute adjustments on his combat ship and P-51, David pumped his bike to St. Ann's Church through tunnels of thinned maples, cut at the top for telephone wires. In the spicy cool darkness, he went to the small white marble altar at the side. Kneeling before Our Lady, he dropped a dime into the metal box on a table of tiered votive candles. As the candles flickered in their red glass cups, David searched for a new one, lit it, and whispered, "Dear Lady, please help me win.'' Later that night, after yet another check of his toolbox, he knelt on the hardwood floor of his darkened bedroom for as long as he could and prayed to God to let him win. Then he climbed into bed, listened to peep frogs, and barely slept.

The morning of the contest the sky was white, and it was hellishly hot. Mike and three other kids, Vic, Nels, and Bobby, arrived early to pick him up. Wearing the club T-shirt with red letters arched over a broken-bladed prop, they carefully stacked the aircraft in the trunk of Mike's big black Buick and were ready to leave when David's mother called him to the house. Cripes, it was for a kiss, so he stalked past her on the porch into the dark hallway, out of sight. After the kiss, she gave him two extra dollars and told him to mind Mr. Brooks—that was Mike.

Once on the road, Mike briefed them on registration procedure, the safety check for all U-Control, and sticking together, pulling for each other as a club. When he spoke of flying, he was dead serious. "When you're flying inverted in Stunt, get right down there on the deck. If you don't—Bobby, you listenin' to me?—If you don't, you lose valuable points, and we're not drivin' all over the state to these contests for nothin'. When you're flyin' Combat, and the guy slips you, wing-over, dive on um, and pull inverted. Remember, you're fightin' the clock. A kill in the first minute of flight is 500 points. Get in the air first, after the Timer says go, get on the other guy's ass, and stay there until that streamer is gone. . . . Another thing, the Bellico brothers. Sure, we all know what they did last year around the state and at the finals BUT, that was that year. All's you gotta do is stay loose. Listen, you guys fly just as good. Don't be ascairt of um. You can beat the piss outta the whole lot if you hafta go against um. Remember that. They ain't Superman. Forget their name, reputation. They're just smart wops that need to be taken down a peg or two. OK?"

"OK."

But David really didn't want to fly Combat. There was no rule that said you had to fly in two events. That was Mike's idea. So David refused to think about it. Instead he sat back and, together with Nels, teased Bobby whom they forced to sit in the middle. They fooled around, giving horse bites, and getting each other in head-locks until Mike yelled to knock it off. Along the highway, there were towering trees, open fields, and farms of postcard beauty divided by stone walls. Above a field, David watched a chicken hawk turning in easy circles, soaring, ready to swoop.

In Canaan, the big black Buick heaved smoothly across the grassy runway of a small rural airport. A man in an olive drab T-shirt, mirror sunglasses, and fatigue cap directed Mike to the end of the field, where another member of the hosting club was forming the cars into aisles. The sun already glinted off several hundred roofs. The grass was flattened, silver, and a faint dust was beginning to rise. Then David's eyes widened, his heart raced. A beautiful yellow free-flight with polyhedral wings buzzed upward on its maximum ten seconds of power, then drifted in great feathery circles, its owner praying, no doubt, for a hot updraft to lengthen its flight. Further off, high above the car roofs, two combat ships dove and nipped at each other's bright-colored, rippling streamers. It was hot, but the air was seasoned with a sweet mist of burned fuel.

Once they found a shady place on the edge of the field, they left their planes and gear and went toward an old, white, barnlike hangar with a gambrel roof. That's where the registration was. The runway moved with gaudy splotches of summer cloth and sunglasses. Contestants had fluttering yellow tickets in belt loops or buttonholes. David was anxious to wear one too. Four or five orange Piper Cubs, real ones, grazed by the hangar in the rich green grass. A big red windsock hung limply, barely stirring, on a tall pole at the south end of the runway. An engine quit and, for a few minutes, there was a strange sun-baked lull.

A smiling man behind the long registration table handed David a yellow ticket and took his money. A girl with piled blond hair entered his name and number on a long list, leaning forward in such a way that he could see into her low-cut dress. The man was saying: "Check your flight time on the blackboard under the tree. Be on time. Listen for your number on the loudspeaker. It's hot. Let's keep the judges in a good mood." Her tanned face turned upward and the long, heavy eyelashes fanned. "Are you flying Combat too?" she asked, the voice husky.

David nodded.

She shuffled through papers and entered his name on another long list. "Thank you very much," she said in the husky voice. "Good luck!"

David smiled, stepped aside. He knotted the yellow I.D. to his

belt loop and waited for Nels and Vic. Under the table were her legs,
warm brown, curving slenderly, one cocked over the other knee,
pumping slowly, up and down.

"Did you enter Combat?" asked Nels.

"Yeah."

"I thought you———"

"I know, I know. Forget it."

Back at their shady encampment, David fussed over his P-51, adjusting the prop so that it would be horizontal to the ground when
the engine quit, cutting down the chance of a nose-over on landing,
the loss of points. Three fellows in white T-shirts stood above him,
hands on hips. They wore shades, tight Levis belted with the buckle
at the side, boots. Their short sleeves were rolled onto the shoulder.
They were dark, oily, with long, swept-back hair. One sucked on a
toothpick and gave David's two aircraft a rotten look, his upper lip
curling away from the teeth. His nose was crooked, and he had big
round eyes, close together. He spat, snuffed. Another one said
"Aero Prop-Busters" in a sissylike way, and together they walked
away laughing. Then Mike squatted next to him. "Those are the
Bellico brothers," he said.

Near the end of the morning, David's number was called for
Stunt. He took his toolbox and carried his P-51 by the cowling to the
judges' table to check in. The red windsock was still motionless.
Good. Nels pumped fuel into the hidden tank while David ran lines
out to the white limed circle, seventy feet away. He checked the up
and down positions of the elevator and ailerons. Nels nodded. After
the judges appraised the aircraft for authentic detail and general ap-
pearance, their pencils moved behind clipboards. David tried to appear casual, but his stomach was tight and icy. If his hand shook,
the flight would be ragged; he'd have no chance at all. *Dear God,
please help me to be still.* The Timer signaled. The engine started
easily, and once David fingered the needle valve to get the right mixture, he lost the dangerous tension. The engine crackled nicely,
notches back from an undesirable scream.

Nels made the release and the blue-gray P-51 with U.S. markings
swept through ten feet of low grass and lifted. A nice takeoff. Three
laps of level flight, waist-high. Good. Everything went fine,

beautiful, until inverted flight when he pulled out from the dive too high and didn't square the corner. Then the three laps of inverted flight were slightly wavered, too far off the deck. By the time he came to the last of the pattern—the square and triangular eights—he was coming apart. The turns weren't sharp. Cripes, he'd be lucky if he got five points on each. And on the overhead stuff, he kept losing the ship in the sun. The engine quit, and he brought her down in a nice slow glide, wind whistling through the cowling and on the taut silk, the wheels touching and the ship rolling to a long stop.

There was scattered applause.

As David reeled in the lines, Bobby ran toward him. "Guess what?" he said, breathlessly.

"What?"

"You drew Bellico for Combat."

He couldn't believe it and went to the blackboard under the big oak tree next to the hangar. It was there all right, his name next to Nick Bellico, and the image of it held him like ice. After memorizing the flight number, he found himself next to a long white catering van, so he bought a hotdog and Pepsi, even though he wasn't hungry. "I saw one of them fly Combat," said Vic, "and he did eights without even looking at his ship while he was waiting for the other guy to get off the deck."

David's mouth went dry.

"Let's go watch some Radio-Control," said Bobby.

"Yeah, c'mon," said Vic.

They walked slowly past the Stunt circle where a big green Thunderbird was going through maneuvers, making precise turns, smooth sweeping arabesques, its engine throating out a beautiful silk drone. David realized now that he had little or no chance in Stunt. The only hope was Combat, but he tried not to think, tried to erase from his mind those bold round eyes, that crooked nose, the cool-guy manner. As they crossed the field, the scent of burned fuel and the sight of several gliders, blue and red, turning and soaring above, had a calming effect. Then he began to laugh with the others at a fat kid who was climbing a tree at the edge of the woods; his plane was stuck at the top and no amount of shaking would free it.

Suddenly the loudspeaker barked and asked everyone to please leave the short east-west runway for a moment to allow a plane to land. The plane, a yellow Piper Cub, grew larger and larger, banked over the trees, glided in for a quiet landing, then throttled noisily to the gas pumps at the old white hangar. David watched a foot emerge and grope for the strut. Then the man, tall and blond, swung out.

"Wouldn't it be something if he came over here and asked us if we wanted a ride?"

"Keep dreaming," said Nels.

The possibility enchanted David, and for a while he felt happy, buoyant. Then came the metallic loudspeaker summons. His heart dove.

Bellico, the youngest one, Nick, appeared at the judges' table with a beautiful, shiny gray Stuka. "You gonna fly *that?*" asked one amazed little kid with freckles.

"Yeah," said Bellico with a smirk.

"What if you crack it up?"

"Never happen."

A Stunt ship, the Stuka that Bellico had flown that morning was a masterpiece: glossy lacquer finish, black swastika decals on the wings and thin round aft section of the fuselage (no seams), long two-seat cockpit, tiny pilot and gunner, wheel skirts, full panel of instruments, and even the antenna wire from cockpit to the small square rudder. David couldn't believe it. How could you fly your best ship in Combat? All that work. A Combat ship was different— you could knock one together in a day or two.

"You must be kidding," said David.

Bellico sucked on his toothpick. "Yeah?" He winked to his brother.

David said, in a voice which surprised him, "OK, your funeral."

Bellico snorted. "Hey, Tony, hear that?"

"Yeah," said the other. They laughed.

"Come on, kiddo," said Bellico, giving David a dark look. "I can't wait for this funeral."

They lined up the two ships and ran out the lines to the white circle, making sure that both black U-Reely handles were even.

"Ever fly Combat, kid?"

David said yes. He could barely keep his hands still.

Bellico snuffed. "Good, glad to hear it."

The field was nearly blind with sunlight. David felt dizzy. He was aware of faces, a large crowd, voices, buzzing engines. Mike was patting his shoulder. "Dave, don't tense up. Remember, stay on top." Nels was mechanic and had fueled the ship—a stubbier, lighter, more maneuverable ship than the Stuka. *Dear God, please let me win.* The Timer shouted: "Ready?"

"Ready," said Bellico.

"Ready," said David.

He jerked the stopwatch and yelled: "Wind 'em up!"

David flipped the prop on his reliable Fox 35, and it caught. He adjusted the gas mixture, yanked the battery clips from the glow plug and venturi, and dashed out to the handle. Motion drained off the tension, and Nels hand-launched the ship. Everything was fine: the engine snarled evenly, and David was first in the air. He took her directly overhead and into a tight circle so that she seemed to be stirring the sky. The sun was going backward. Finally, he heard the Stuka's engine, a different pitch, and saw Bellico running out. David dove his ship to a place just behind the launch point and did eights, waiting. It was legal, but Bellico said, "Come on, you bastid, move!" But David held. Then Nick signaled his brother to launch.

The shiny gray Stuka leaped into the air, swastikas flashing. David bumped shoulders with Bellico, made his pass, and cut only a small piece of the streamer. A cut, not a kill. He'd blown it and would need a miracle to get him again. They staggered, round and round, in a small circle, arms extended, trying to keep the handles even. The sun went backward. Diving and nipping, the aircraft buzzed like saws in the heat. David was dizzy again. He made a wingover, planning to dive on the Stuka at the other side, but at the top of the circle, directly overhead, both planes were for a second held frozen, then seemed to explode in the sun so that David didn't even see his ship cut the Stuka's streamer six inches from the rudder as Bellico swerved. They grunted and puffed, struggling to untangle the lines. Bellico's frenzied elbow caught David in the jaw and knocked him on his back. The lines jerked. "You little bastid," hissed Bellico, his lines cut. David scrambled to his feet, saving his ship at the last moment. Then he caught a glimpse of the Stuka as it left the circle, climbed, and made for the woods behind the hangar, where it suddenly dove out of sight.

David's heart pounded, out of excitement, not fear. He felt good and, flying out the remainder of his tank, did loops and crazy fluttering eights. Cocky, no longer dizzy, he flew the plane by touch, looking away toward the crash where Bellico was running, followed by a trickle of kids. As Nels ducked his way out, David became aware of cheering and clapping. "Hey, you might have it wrapped up. A cut and kill. You got the kill in forty-two seconds. That's 510 points," said Nels. "Man, that's gonna be tough to beat. . . . Hey, I think the crowd's glad you got Bellico."

Later, after most of the Combat had been flown, and David was sure of First Place, he walked toward the Bellico encampment. He wanted to apologize, generously, of course, and to see what had happened to the Stuka. The sun was nearly down, but David's arms and neck were already burned. There were still some spectators in a thin ring. The Stuka was a shattered pile of balsa, torn silk, dangling lead-out wires. Only the wingtips and tail section were intact. David thought of a smashed pheasant he had once seen on the road, an explosion of feathers, no form. Looking at the Stuka, he experienced a sad thrill. Then he approached and said he was sorry. The kid bounced to his feet, his face dark red, eyes teary. "You little bastid, get outta here," he growled, "or I'll kick your ass." He came at David with clenched fists, but his father, a short man with a gravel voice, stepped between. "You betta go," he said.

"All's I ——— "

"That's OK, kid, you betta go."

II

As rain begins to break on the windshield, David finds a filling station. Steam leaks from the grill, and he can barely see the man who directs him, left then right, into an empty bay. The place stinks of gunk and grease. Away for two years, nearly home, now this. The mechanic lifts the hood and leans to the side of the steam. "It's the lower hose," he says. David is drawn by the dark face and large round eyes that crowd the man's nose—a nose that is crooked, broken. "It shouldn't take more than ten minutes or so."

"Thanks."

From the office, he studies the face. There should be a nameplate over the lintel, he thinks, and steps under the overhang, turning, craning his neck. There it is: NICK BELLICO, PROPRIETOR. Rain pours out of the dark sky and beats the tar into silver.

David stands in the station office, watching the rain and seeing, in that fallen summer night, a small face, red, angry, unforgiving. Remembering also his mother and father, taut with pride, as he came through the kitchen door with the big gold trophy, David now thinks of soon being with them, older and wrinkled, but still proud of him, still happy to see him. The car trunk is full of gifts he has brought from Japan.

"That oughta 'bout do it," says Bellico, wiping his hands on a rag. David hands him a credit card. Bellico's face seems too old for its age. Two front teeth are missing. The jawbone is hidden, padded with flesh. As he fills out the slip, David tells him who he is. Bellico looks up, tilts his head, and the eyes light. He slaps the desk. "How do ya like that? Sure it's you! I didn't recognize ya with that mustache."

David tells him about Canaan, that it was his first contest, that he was sort of pushed into Combat and had beginner's luck. He has a sudden urge to tear himself down.

"Hell," says Bellico, "you got real good, real fast. You took two or three other firsts that summer, as I remember." He laughs, bobs his head. "Man, I got mad that day."

"Why did you ever fly that Stuka?"

"Ahh, I was a show-off, ya know? I thought I could bluff ya. Hey, as a kid, ya pull some crazy shit, ya know?"

David agrees. A red Pontiac rolls to the pumps and rings the bell. Bellico ducks through the rain, puts the nozzle in the tank spout, and leaves it on automatic.

David asks, "Did you ever fly a real plane?"

Bellico pushes the slip across the desk for David to sign. "No, you?"

"No," says David, surprised at the lie.

"Me neither, man, I keep both feet on the ground."

"How's your father? I remember he used to go to all the contests with you."

The voice softens. "Passed away a few years back."

"I'm sorry."

"Cancer."

"How about your brothers? They ever fly any more?"

"Nah, they're married, like me, kids, tied down. One of my little cousins, though, is into Radio Control. That's the thing now, ya know? Practically no more U-Control. Hey, like everything else, more . . . scientific, ya know? And they fly Combat with them things too."

A horn sounds at the pumps.

Bellico groans and makes a gesture at the car. He tears the blue carbon away and gives David a copy. "Man, I'm gonna tell my brothers I saw you. Small world, huh?" He extends his dirty hand and David takes it. "Good luck to ya," he says.

And steps into the rain.

"You too," yells David. He stares at the wet footprints on the cement floor, at the empty space.

Rain beats against the windshield. The wipers click at top speed, and still there are barely two hundred feet of visible road. Telephone wires and treetops blur, sharpen, blur, sharpen. It is like flying blind and having to depend on his instruments and the carrier radio that crackles the directions as he hunts that small, dry moving spot in the vast South China Sea, Hanoi flakpuff black and still popping in his mind's eye. Why had he lied? He does something Bellico would give anything to do. The danger. The excitement. The sense of brotherhood. Nick Bellico. David had extended his hand, and now it is gritty and smeared with rust that thins and reddens but won't rub off on the handkerchief. He doesn't want to think but sees a montage of aircraft going back to the cemetery and the gliders, and beyond. How beautiful they were, hanging, slowly turning, exploding, and reappearing out of the sun. But somehow David feels sad, heavy, ashamed. He is frightened. He sees a man's body lying in an open sunny field. The torso is bare, a huge bloody cavity. David feels something swoop at his chest; he feels as if his heart is in the clutch of talons.

In a Field of Force

His mother cupped her palm over the mouthpiece and aimed the black receiver at his chest. "Gino," she said in a thin reedy whisper, "you talk to him and be civil."

He slowly backed from the phone. Christ, he did not want to talk to Father Mellon, especially now. Mellon was all capital letters, a list of prohibitions.

"Gino, I never ask very much of you."

"Ma, Kathy's waiting for me in the truck." He watched her eyes go gray and blunt like the heads of two bullets. He sighed and grabbed the phone. Over a bad connection, he exchanged greetings with Mellon, whose smooth voice asked if the campus trouble had been as bad as the media said it was.

"Worse," said Gino, refusing to elaborate. He knew his mother monitored darkly from the doorway.

Father Mellon went on about Truth: "It's hard, very hard to find. The Left says one thing and the Right says another. I think of Babel these days. Remember, honest men can be at opposite sides of the fence." Gino nibbled at the dead skin on his lips. His cheeks were hot. Outside the window were starlings in the snow; they pecked at each other for the seed his father had left on the ground. "Truth, in the last analysis, is a chameleon." Static crackled on the line. There was a long pause.

Gino strained to respond, changed the subject. "Given any good sermons lately?" he asked without bothering to hide his irony.

There came a lofty chuckle. "Yes, as a matter of fact, a good one on the Pill."

"In which, of course, you considered all sides of the issue."

"But the Church's position is firm on this point."

Gino scoffed. "I thought Truth was a chameleon."

Mellon laughed. "You confuse faith and politics. We'll have to discuss that one. Listen, I won't keep you. Do come up some night while you're home. We'll have some coffee. Bring your wife; I'd like to meet her."

"We'll see."

"Well, so long. Merry Christmas." There was a pause. Mellon breathed, waited, and Gino returned with a simple "Goodbye."

His mother reappeared smiling. "There, that didn't kill you, did it?"

The road ran ahead for almost a mile along the river. In the cold gray water, ice floes were slowly drifting toward the drawbridge. Up river in the cove, he used to dig clams with his father, but now it was posted. The boatyard was full of hauled yachts and thick with masts. So many gold-lettered sterns. Mellon's sailboat was among them. Gino had been out in it once because he served well and knew his Latin.

Kathy said, "You don't like anyone, do you?"

He stared at the road.

"What's wrong with Father Mellon?"

"If you had to suffer the bastard through twelve years of school, you wouldn't have to ask."

"Oh, puke. That's no answer." She folded her arms and squinted at a snowbound farm.

There was a brittle quiet. Slowing for the turn onto the bridge, Gino could see the bay, a vast sheet of corrugated tin. The muffler of the old pickup gurgled and popped. The tires whined on the metal roadway, and the bridge struts flew back. Then it was quiet except for an occasional ping from the truck's heater.

After another five miles, near the crest of a final hill, Gino down-shifted, and the city slid into view. Hotel Algonquin was still the tallest structure, then the steeples of churches, their crosses dull gold in the haze. Across the river were the giraffelike cranes in the ship-yard where Polaris subs were made.

"You're still angry, aren't you?" Kathy asked.

Gino shook his head. She was trying to draw him out, to keep him buoyant. There was a lot he would have to adjust to.

"So we had an accident," said Kathy, "but at least we can afford it."

Gino tightened his grip on the wheel. Sure they could afford it. But what about the summer? The plans for camping and traveling?

"Come on," she coaxed, her expression sunny. "I'm not even sure yet. I've been late before."

He nodded. A child would surely please his mother, perhaps his father too. There had been hints. News about high school friends. Oh, so and so just had another. Three that makes it. Yes, he wanted to say, three the world doesn't need. But he said nothing, his jaw muscles tight.

At the bottom of the hill, they joined a slow-moving line of traffic. Now there were cars behind them. They were locked in. It would be like this all the way to the center of town. Two kids in a new Dodge with high rearend and wide tires were clowning around. The driver pumped the brakes so that the car rocked violently and a row of red lights blasted on and off. Gino gnawed at his thumbnail and flew the piece from his tongue. His face broiled.

"Can we?"

"Can we what?" asked Gino.

"Aren't you listening? I asked if we could go to Mass this year? It's not to bug you, but last year was awful. All the drinking at Eddie's, no Christmas tree, no church. It just wasn't Christmas. Going to a bar and getting smashed isn't my idea. . . . " Folding her arms, she looked away.

Gino chewed at the skin on his lip. The cab was close and moist with the rusty warmth of the heater. His neck began to prickle. He cracked the window slightly. Cars creeped and spurted. He continued to shift from first to second and back to first. The transmission whined a complaint as they moved past service stations and used car lots, each with huge electric signs.

Next to the blackened wall of an old furniture warehouse was a newly made vacant lot with a string of red, blue, and yellow bulbs that went around the perimeter. A sign, jerkily painted, said:

V.F.W. XMAS TREES. He waited for her to see it. Then she did and a
smile bloomed on her face. He pulled from the line of traffic.
"Look at all the pretty trees," she said, imitating the wonderment
of a child. She laughed and jumped from the truck. The snow was
covered with needles and twigs from the cut evergreens that filled
the lot. Some were tied and stacked, others were leaning against
temporary fences. Each had a white price tag that fluttered in the icy
wind. A bearish red-faced man in a plaid hunting jacket staggered
from a small shack. His eyes popped and had tiny red threads on the
white. Silver claws poked out from the loose plaid sleeves.

"Got some nice trees," he said.

"We're just looking around," said Gino.

But the man continued to follow them, to press closely. They went
up and down the aisles, sized up the trees. Only the extra-large were
full-boughed, the others skeletal. Some had fallen from the poised
upright position against the fence. Their undersides were white like
the bellies of floating fish. In the street, an old car honked like a
goose. The red-faced man picked up a fallen tree for Gino to judge.
"Big or small house?" he slurred.

"Big," said Gino, catching the man's sour breath.

He snorted in disgust and pushed the tree roughly on its side.

The ritual of getting a tree disappeared for Gino after the eighth
grade. Too much bother, said his parents. But yesterday, with Dad,
he trudged through deep snow into the woods behind the barn. With
pick and shovel, he searched for a suitable spruce or fir that he in-
tended to dig up, roots and all, and replant in the yard come spring.
But he found nothing that would look quite right. The best trees
were on the other side of the new turnpike, which bisected the farm.
It was too cold and the snow too deep. As they stood by the woven
wire fence and watched a diesel tractor-trailer shift on the hill, then
blackly cough itself over the crest, he asked his father's opinion of
the new road and got a shrug for an answer.

In a more intimate moment Gino asked what Dad had thought
about the prospect of having a child. Did he remember the details?
Did the responsibility scare him? Another shrug. A puzzled look.
Then: "You're a father, you work, you provide. That's it." In his
voice there was a hint of pique. Gino was ashamed. Maybe he

shouldn't have tried. On the way back to the house, he pictured a tiny fetus beginning to grow in Kathy's womb. He could hear trucks groaning loudly on the pike. God, nothing ever stayed still.

The red-faced man picked up another tree. "Nothin' wrong wit dis one," he growled. It had two missing branches and looked like a pole. "Go great in a corner."

Gino shook his head.

In the truck, they waited to cut into traffic. Sweat trickled down Gino's ribcage. Christ, none of the cars would break to let him in. The red-faced man, miffed and glaring, stood near the front bumper and barked: "You could of bought one, you little piss ant!"

Gino peeled rubber. "I should have run him down," he gritted.

"Gino! Don't talk that way."

They pulled off the main road and drove for ten minutes, turning left and right and going through a number of busy intersections. This time they were on a street with tall trees, and there was a sign that read: CHRISTMAS TREES: LIVE AND CUT. In the front yard were two large maples with branches that arched over the house. From an old red lean-to at the side hung wreaths and sprays of holly. Several families were looking hopefully in and out of the rows. A boy with long red hair that escaped from beneath a blue stocking cap lagged behind them. Probably a high school kid. He was working a wad of gum and had traces of acne. He slouched, was indifferent, and laughed for some obscure reason. "You like this baby?" he asked and pointed to a tree with roots bundled in burlap. "Lotta people gettin' these now."

"How much are they?" asked Kathy.

"Most of them are twelve," he said and lifted his brow. "But figure you can dig 'em up every year."

Gino looked at Kathy. "Let's get one," he said. Excitement spread in her eyes like sunlight on open water. They searched for a good one. Most were giant or runty, but soon they found one that was perfect. It was a spruce, thickly green and conical. Nearly six and a half feet tall. Gino and the boy staggered and grunted with the tree until it rested on the bed of the truck. The needles squeaked on the rear window of the cab. "I don't want to bend the boughs," he told the boy as he paid him. From under the ripped driver's seat, he took a length of white nylon cord and tied the tree to the wooden headboard.

"Now," she said, apologetically. "One more thing?"

"What's that?"

"I need a few things at the Mall."

He bit his cheek, shifted, and headed across town. Using all the side streets and short cuts he knew, he drove fast, downshifting and braking hard. Twice there were ONE WAY signs on streets that were formerly two way. His face was hot and his undershirt soaked. He moistened his lips. They had to hurry. The first shift at the shipyard would soon be out. Traffic would be even worse on the way home.

The Mall had a huge parking lot, but from the cloverleaf overpass he could see there was no space. Thousands of car roofs reflected the weak hazy sun. Gino decided to park on the other side of the highway. The truck would be pointed in a homeward direction. They could cross to the Mall on foot. It was downhill, too, and he could keep an eye on the tree.

"I'll wait here," he said and stood just inside the door.

"Okay, I'll be about ten minutes."

By the enormous plate glass wall, he watched her disappear in the tide of shoppers. Christmas carols rang tinnily from speakers along the concourse. There was a roped-off Santa receiving kids with hopeful faces; one by one they told him their wants.

Outside the door, an old yellow Pontiac with body rot and broken exhaust idled roughly and discharged a mother and five children. The mother was wrapped in a faded blue coat, her hair in curlers covered by a white scarf. Her face was puffy and dark and had a cigarette tucked into a corner of the red mouth. Gino watched her waddling toward him, herding her chicks through the door.

The concourse roared. The truck, small and green, sat on the hill. Twice, several cars slowed suspiciously past. Where was she? The shipyard would be letting out any minute. Gino hurried down the concourse. Jostled by the crowd past Santa, he made his way to the store. He walked down an aisle that was narrowed by boxes of extra stock. Shelves, heavily piled, rose almost to the ceiling. He turned left, then right and at last came to a clearing. A fake evergreen stood before him; it was seven feet high and looked almost real. The boughs were made of twisted wire segments, each like a green bottle brush. A printed card proclaimed: IT WILL LAST FOREVER: $15.00. He could still see their tree on the bed of the truck. Two men were probably lifting it onto another pickup. Christ, where the hell was she? He was walking, looking, rising on his toes. From the left came the sound of chirping birds. Canaries and parakeets.

"Excellent price on that table. Ten percent off." The voice was deep, husky. The man, broad-shouldered, fashionably dressed, and wearing gold-rimmed glasses, rocked on his heels.

"I'm just looking for my wife," murmured Gino.

"What?" His sideburns were like knives, his trousers sharply creased. He was all edges and too close for Gino, who moved away and looked down an aisle to the right where there were gold and silver cages in tiers. Gino's face felt red. He bit at the skin on his lip. "What did you have in mind?" The salesman stationed himself in Gino's view, feet apart, rocking on his heels. His hands, big and hairy, glittering with rings, wiped his mouth, then cradled the chin.

"My wife, now bug off."

"What? I can't hear you."

The canaries cheeped louder. Past the salesman's shoulder they were moving yellow blurs. Gino's ears rang. He averted his eyes, turned, and walked away.

A little boy with dark curly hair stood in the aisle holding a toy rifle. Gino stopped. It was a replica of the M-16. The boy looked up, placed it back in the box, and ran off. Gino's hands went out and brought it back; they closed around the grips and remembered the feel. Nearly the same size, though much lighter than his .22 Winchester, long unused, home rusting in the shed. This was made of plastic but surprisingly real with the sling and square magazine on the underside. Gino gazed down the aisle and saw the woman with the faded blue coat and white scarf. The coat was open now, and he could see that her stomach bulged with an unborn child. The raggy children flocked about her legs and tugged at her skirt. She scolded them in a foreign language. They were probably Puerto Ricans. The husband was with them now; he was wearing a leather jacket and gray T-shirt, hair tufting from the collar, a gold chain around his neck. One of the children began to stare at Gino. She had pigtails

tied with bright red ribbon and wore a coat that was too big. The
face was dirty and the nose ran freely. Nearby were cash registers
chugging up sales. The sound grew louder and louder. Things
bought and soon discarded by people like this. So many of them all
over the country breeding mountains of garbage. With a fresh butt
in her mouth, the mother, child in her arms, also began to stare at
Gino. Finally all of their eyes were on him. He threw off the safety
and cut loose with the M-16, blew the baby from the woman's arms.
Her mouth, round and moaning, was a ruby hole. The long cigarette, from her lower lip, fell end over end. The rifle bucked against
his shoulder. He fired again and watched her fly against a shelf, raking dozens of dolls to the floor. The dirty children were lifted from
the ground like puppets on a wire. The father shook his head,
pleadingly extended his hand, then shot backward with another
burst. He lay on his back, a pink stain spreading and reddening on
his shirt. The noise was terrible, yet Gino fired again. The bodies
jumped with the entering of each slug. He whirled to cover his back.
The salesman stood in the mouth of the aisle, his jaw slack. Gino
gave him a burst, too, and watched him bounce against a stack of
boxes that toppled and buried him so that only his legs were in sight.
The ringing finally subsided. Again he could hear the tropical birds,
the cash register still on a binge.

"What are you doing with that?" asked Kathy.

Gino looked down at the rifle. "Nothing," he said, putting it
back in the box.

"Let's get going," she said, handing him some lip ice. "Here,
your lip is bleeding."

The truck tires moaned on the metal roadway of the bridge, and
Gino's stomach was tight; it felt as if a piece of ice had left the river
and lodged in his belly. He kept seeing the family, the woman lying
on her back, her head oddly twisted, blood leaking from the nose.
The jungle birds were making a din.

At last he drove up the long dirt road between the two front fields.
The house was white clapboard with black shutters. There was a barn
and a shed, both weathered to the color of an old beehive. A wall of
trees stood in back and at the side of the house. His father, a slight

man with a leathery face, gray hair, and smiling eyes, came out to help, and together they worried the tree into the front hall.

"How much did it cost?" asked Mom.

"Twelve dollars," said Kathy.

"My Lord," said Mom, "we used to pay a dollar. Remember, Dad?" She turned around. "Now where did he go?"

"To get some floor covering, I guess."

She turned to Kathy. "That husband of mine," she said jokingly, "spends more time in the barn, the yard, and the Lord knows where. Goes out with the trash and stands there looking at the trees like he's never seen them before. What you'd call a real Nature Boy."

Kathy laughed and conspired. "My father's something like that too," she said.

"Is he? Well, I'm a city girl. I may be here, but my heart's right down there at the corner of State and Main." She paused and looked more closely at the tree. "Well, dear, what are you going to put on the limbs?"

Gino left the room and went to the shed. The door window still showed the two BB holes from his early teens. He put his fingertips to the rough round craters. His father moved quietly in the semidark and when he bent to retrieve something on a lower shelf, the crossed mullions seemed to rest on his back. Finally he emerged with a folded canvas. "Should do," he said, and they walked back to the house.

Gino and his father set the tree on canvas and stepped back to see it poised between the two front windows. Too close to the radiator. They moved it more to the side. That was better. But Gino would still have to spray the limbs now and then with water from a Windex bottle to make sure they didn't dry out. Kathy was telling his father that the ornaments would be strung popcorn and cranberries, candy canes and snowman cookies with white glazed frosting. Nothing electric. She said that the stringing would take time, and everyone had to help. His father laughed and gave her a hug. Gino studied the tree. They must not put too much weight on the branches. He tested their spring, the needles prickly to the touch, then smelled the resin on his fingers.

In the kitchen his mother was preparing supper, and Kathy was popping corn for the tree; she shook the pan, and kernels exploded like gunfire. Gino winced, took a bottle of beer from the refrigerator, and prized off the cap. His mother gave him a dark look. His drinking had caused her pain in the past.

The glassed-in porch, which ran the length of two sides of the house, was warmed by the sun even in winter. It was always comfortable until after dark. Gino sat in a chaise lounge, sipped his beer, and gazed at a red streak of sun on the snow. He followed with his eye the set of tracks he and his father had made into the trees yesterday afternoon. *You're a father, you work, you provide. That's it.* He put down the beer and took up the Russian novel he had been trying to read. Overhead, a very slight draft tinkled the glass mobile.

Kathy came out to the porch, straddled the chair, and sat on his thighs. The corners of her mouth lifted into a smile. Her teeth were even and very white. But what would they be like when the fetus began to draw on her calcium? Dark from the loss. And what of the color in her cheeks? The baby with its secret needs would take that too. She leaned down until their foreheads touched. The plain gold cross he had given her as a birthday gift slipped from her blouse and dangled near his face. He let his eye travel the chain to her dark throat and then to her eyes, round and sea blue. "Your Mom and Dad are in a great mood," she said. "We'll have a good time tonight, OK?"

"OK," he said. There was a moment of quiet, then Gino said, "I was thinking we might go to midnight Mass tomorrow."

"Fine," she said. Her expression was warm with love, approval. Yet his head felt loosely on, the skull bone fragile. If bumped, it would roll from his shoulders, crack open on the floor, and his thoughts would wriggle out in their slime for her or anyone else to see. He wanted to confess but couldn't. Someday maybe but not now. He would have to find a way.

"We're going to be eating pretty soon," she said, kissed him softly on the mouth and went inside.

"Please forgive me," he whispered.

The mobile tinkled as if in response. He watched the quarter moon come up in the east. The trees were dark against the snow, and a single birch, aslant, glowed palely amid the rest. He picked up the novel. At first he read slowly, his mind refusing to give in; then it no longer balked, and he was in a world of icons, monks, peasants, and endless wheat-rippled steppes. "Tachanka," "moujik," and other strong new words came now and then to his eyes—God-bringing words, like the Latin prayers he had learned as a boy.

How It Fee-yuls

In the clear bathroom mirror, Konrad's face was not clear; the skin
had the creases of a sat-on raincoat and the eyes were puffy, small,
and red. His hand fumbled for the spigot and bumped into Kiddo's
yellow plastic steamboat. "The hell?" he mumbled and chucked it
into the tub. On the sink ledge where his shaving things usually sat,
there was a splayed, back-broken copy of some Marriage Guide that
Linda was reading; it was written by two Ph.D.s and prefaced by
another. Konrad grunted, gave it a Frisbee snap, and sent it—minus
a few down-fluttering pages—into the living room where Kiddo lay
inches from the color cartoons: loud nasal dialogue, zooms, boings,
and block-buster whistles. The face in the mirror tried to focus, ap-
praise its reddish cheek stubble, the full chevron of a mustache, the
thick wiry hair that balled out into an amber-blond afro. Not bad.
He was satisfied, more than satisfied. It was important to like
yourself, and Konrad did. Inhaling deeply, closing his eyes, he men-
tally saw his buddy, the Hark, who was into high energy because he
liked himself and knew his body. Konrad wiggled his toes, caressed
his delts and pecks, fingered his parts. It was axiomatic: if you were
into your body, could your head be far behind?

Konrad picked up the green soap from its white plastic dish and
part of his dream came back, the green water. It was . . . Konrad
tried to think what it was. "I had this dream," he impulsively yelled
from the bathroom. He listened. From the bedroom, a faint groan.

"Daddy watch tee-wee wif me?" And Kiddo looked up hopefully
from Konrad's pink knobby knee.

"Right." He backed from the mirror for an angle peek into the bedroom. In a saffron nightie, Linda sat jack-knifed on her heels at the foot of the bed.

"DADDY!"

"Hey, cool it. Gimme a minute."

Konrad watched her fingers dive backward into long blond hair. Her small breasts quivered, like bait.

"I had this heavy dream."

"I'm all ears." Linda slid from the bed. Out of sight, she did not exist, and Konrad needed eye contact, an adoring audience for his dream-tale. But Linda was rattling hangers in the closet. The dream was. . . . His face worked in the mirror but words would not form themselves. So forget it. Besides, overexposed in his marriage, Konrad felt a new need to keep secrets. If he told her that the Hark was in his dream, she would sniff and say, "That doesn't surprise me at all." And surprise, the Hark used to say, was where it was at, was what made getting out of bed (or into one!) worth it. A gift you owed to your Self. Konrad gave himself a wide grin. "Oh Hark, you are definitely a heavy dude."

After several cups of thick black coffee in order to pick up speed, Konrad began his ritual of observing, re-observing, or noticing. It was important to see things, really notice, no matter how lowly they might seem—like the blistered ribs of the radiator, the way it whistled, sputtered, bonked. Or how the ceiling was low, and the eaves fell sharply on all sides. Konrad eyed the furniture—furniture he insisted be basic and secondhand, even rough. Linda complained, but he was a purist on the point and eventually every item came from Good Will, Catholic Charities, or garage sales. After the seedy apartment had been scoured and painted, Linda introduced, one by one, her uncanny "finds": a wine-colored Persian prayer rug, an old gate-leg made of walnut, cable-spool end tables, a buttoned leather sofa with rips nicely stitched, a Bentwood rocker with a re-webbed seat (newly painted), and a butterfly chair. Later came the two ladderbacks, antiques, only wanting a few hours work. Konrad felt uneasy. From junk Linda had created an apartment that was warm, comfortable. Almost as if she had beat him by his own rules.

He looked at it: a lovely nest. And clean. Her neatness depressed him. And the originals and reproductions her art major friends had given flung him into an unspoken twit. Sometimes he felt that something—he couldn't say what exactly—but something he had tried desperately to avoid was being accomplished nonetheless. "Christ, a good thing the Hark hauled ass for Canada."

"What?"

"Nothing."

Konrad studied the rivering grain in a floorplank at the rug edge; it divided around a black knot. But that he had seen before and aside from not being able to relate it especially to his own life-style, he knew it was more important to notice something new, something ready to pounce and surprise. He got down on the floor to gulliver about with Kiddo, who climbed all over him, jumped on his chest, got bored, and returned to the irresistible beep-beep of the Road-runner. Konrad liked this one, too. When he was at school, he and the Hark used to do dope and watch cartoons and soap operas. Hark had a color TV in his room, and on weed or dex the colors smouldered inside your skull. For laughs, they would drag a magnet across the screen to stretch and warp faces, turn people green or orange, have whiteouts, squeeze the image. On the right stuff, it was a giddy fun house trip. But the Hark said soap was the art of the people, revolutionary. Foreign flicks and art galleries were bour-geois. Marriage too. But here there was no hassle because one time, after two hits of electric kool-aid, Konrad saw in the Hark's red mind, as skull matter melted like a doll's face held too close to a flame, an image of himself and Linda and a side-long pickerel smile and Hark's eyes close soundlessly, said it was their own thing, therefore cool.

On his back, Konrad looked at the tall gauzy rectangle of the cur-tained window. The room had a sky of cracked plaster; it was covered, in part, by wallpaper that had been painted. The best part, in Konrad's mind, was the corner where a brown water stain spread toward the center light fixture. A stain which looked like—looked like what? Konrad tried to think. A nose. A boot maybe. Italy. The tip almost touching Greece. Then, lying as he was on his back, he spied something chalked on the underside of the gate-leg, the espial of which opened his mouth in wonder. A graffito: SKORK. What the hell was that? He was almost telling Linda when he caught himself, pleased both with his self-control and the new thing noticed, the secret. SKORK. It could be foreign. "Definitely far-out."

But life was still low on its wick. The day was cold, sleety; it was the color of dishwater, matrimonially grim. Konrad went to the window. There was a psychedelic red river that came from the steel mill—a "working river," they called it. At night the sky was a glowing red, the air smelled of sulphur. Linda wanted to move. Konrad said he wasn't going to some bourgeois suburb. No way. Air with a whiff of rotten eggs told you where reality was; here there was more contact with life. Besides, Konrad liked the house. In a storm, he liked to stand in the old bow window and think of the house as an old rust-bucket freighter. He would jostle the suspended hurricane lamp in the alcove as he faced the storm head on. The old man, his landlord, and dog were in steerage below. The Hark had put him onto a poem where this kid sails a greenhouse through a stormy night into the morning with a full cargo of roses. Most far-out poem he had ever read. Roses. The day, though, was darkening and getting to him, and he felt like cutting out. Two years ago at this time, alone, he had driven up to Toronto. In a week, he and the Hark had done some crazy drugs, talked about school, the war, Nixon's pig trip. They went to a restaurant with Julie, a girl Hark was living with. In candle flicker, Hark told of his plans to cut out for Greece, Crete, the Aegean. Julie's eyes sprang wide, misted. "This is news," she said, her mouth doing funny twitches. Hark had already bought his ticket and was leaving in a week. Julie pushed back her chair: "Why don't you just stab me?" Hark said, "We agreed it wasn't a forever thing, right?" Her whole face was working, the eyes were freaky. "WHY DON'T YOU FUCKING STAB ME?" she screamed, then fled. Bad trip. Turning heads. But Hark poured on the wine. He looked at Konrad calmly. "We agreed on doing our own thing, you know? Now she pulls this Hollywood number." His grin spread like syrup. "Fuck it, right?" And up went the glasses of dark red wine.

The white-and-blue postal jeep splashed up the pot-holed street. Television noise had begun to add to Konrad's dispeace and made him glad for the possibility of mail. Several weeks ago, the Hark had planted a fresh image of himself in Konrad's mind with a postcard from Náxos: a fishing village with a vanishing line of caïques along a stone jetty the color of piecrust. Houses were dazzling white, roof tiles orange. Green water. A sun-baked Greek sponge diver with a jet black mustache in the foreground. On the reverse the Hark had printed: "Isles of Homer. Omphalos of all Western hangups. But I'm worshiping the sun, sipping *ouzo,* and studying cat's paws." Konrad didn't exactly know what it meant or what Hark was sipping, but it was far-out. Greek Isles. Hark, that old muvva. Linda sniffed, shook her head, and said it wasn't like the travel posters. Bumming around was sweaty, dirty, hungry, and more often than not, a rip-off trip. She knew, had been all around Europe when her father was stationed in Spain. Konrad ground his teeth.

"It's cold, put on your jacket."

"Sure."

He padded in Apache mocassins down the front stairs and out to the far end of the freezing porch where the mailbox hung cockeyed by one rusty screw. Icy cold gripped his legs and bit his face, its pain lighting his head, bringing him, he felt, more sensation, awareness. Pain was important. Deliberately, he took his shivering time. Box was black, paint chipped, bottom furred with rust. Lid clanked. Konrad plucked two envelopes from the narrow metal pocket, barking his knuckle. "Shit!" One was a bill, the other a letter from Linda's friend, Beth.

The name uncorked his worst spirits. Beth was very untogether as far as Konrad was concerned. She disapproved of dope, was full of second-hand ideas; she was the type who would eat soggy tea bags—string, tab, and all—if a bestseller said you should do it. Konrad climbed the stairs. His mind produced a unisex haircut and a long jaw with a snapping overbite. Memory prickled. First she married, then Linda (Konrad making it different with a J. P.); she got pregnant, then Linda; now she owned a house and just recently Linda had begun this number about moving. Kiddo's eyes went red from the mill and he coughed, she said. Konrad said he would never buy a house. No way. A house was terminal bourgeois, the last trip, a bummer, a capitalist rip-off.

Kiddo was still on the floor, aimed at the cartoons. Linda, slung in the yellow butterfly chair, was reading *The Closing Circle,* a book Beth had yammered about one day last summer. Not that Konrad didn't like to read; he loved Gnossos and Dangerfield and how they fucked over the straights and the gullible. They were beautiful. There were scenes he read over and over. And the characters, for Konrad, were not characters; they were blood-real, like the freaks he and Hark knew at State. But Beth had to analyze the shit out of everything. Once, he told her his favorite poem and when he said the last several lines of it, she wanted to know what it meant, "a cargo of roses"? Konrad went to the kitchen to make coffee or something and heard her saying " . . . would seem to indicate . . . suggest . . . not sure it couldn't be regarded as a deep image. . . . " She was gesturing with a cigarette, smoking herself into a short circuit of itches, coughs, and hisses. Definitely untogether, Konrad said to himself. Full of stirs, she disapproved of drugs. What a laugh. But let her yatter on; Konrad read the *Ching.* It flowed, took you out of your head, plugged you into high energy. The Hark said it made Western books, the Bible included, look uptight.

Linda uncurled from her book. "What's in the mail?" Konrad flipped the letter into her lap. Linda's face brightened, her fingers tearing a thin strip from the envelope end. Then she blew, puffed it out, and plucked the letter. Silently, her eyes snapped back and forth.

"What's her act?"

"Nothing," said Linda, reading.

"Whaddya mean, nothing?"

"Just what she's doing."

"Reading, you mean."

"Doing and reading, okay?" And her face wrinkled with anger, and Konrad hated it that way. "You're getting so fucking paranoid."

"What else?" Konrad hovered.

"She was thinking maybe we could get together." She said it in a low-key unasking way that maddened him, made him wish she would come right out and yell and scream so he could do the same. Thus, with only a slight change of inflection and volume did he say, "No way."

"Just a few days."

"No way."

"*One* day, for chrissakes. Would it kill you?"

"No. fucking. way."

Konrad saw a double threat: Beth was bad enough but her husband—he was slight and had delicate hands carved out of soap, a tentative beard, and a little mustache the color of shit. He taught sociology and was an expert on everything. He had all the right things: a little backyard garden, two ten-speeds, two kids, and a toy terrier that did a nightly poo-poo on the end of a leash. Of theories, he had many, was always yapping about his book, a book he was writing on morality, television, and mass opinion. It came as no surprise to Konrad that he believed and drunkenly tried to argue that the baseball curve was an illusion.

Everything became tense and quiet. Kiddo always whimpered at yelling. Konrad reflected in the alcove at the helm. The Hark had always said, "Consider the trip." And the trip right now was going poorly. Konrad at length reneged, outlined a workable solution: "Be cool, okay? Let's not hassle each other. It's open, right? Do our own thing. When we come to the bridge, we'll cross it. Respect each other's thing, right? What else can I say?"

Linda was incredulous.

"What's the matter?"

"Oh wow!"

Konrad put his arm around her.

"You won't visit my parents. You———"

"Cut the shit, hunh? It's one thing or the other. Not both."

"I don't get it."

"Beth or the Colonel? I'm not wasting my vacation with visiting and the whole fucking trip."

"Vacation? You're not even working!"

"So what? It's still a holiday, right?"

"Oh wow!"

"Hey, day after Christmas I start tending at Rude Willy's."

"Big deal." Linda was white. Kiddo whined and tugged her jeans. "Mama, I hungwe." Linda's chest heaved. "If——" she began.

"HUNG—WEE!"

They shed their clothes. Konrad put on his headphones and Linda hers. With Kiddo safely down for a nap, Konrad carefully began to prepare for himself a rosy blissfulness. From beneath the carpet he produced a joint previously rolled and slyly stashed for the occasion. "Presto," he said. Linda laughed. With motorcycle glasses, long ash-blond hair, she was still, even after Kiddo, a little stick of a girl. It pleased Konrad that she was like one of those toy balloons that bubble out and deflate into their original shape. That was Linda. She took a deep toke and passed off. He was beginning to feel it already and drew in so greedily that his face quivered, got the color of cranberry juice. For the remaining sliver, Konrad got out his roach-clip, sniffed and sucked at every stray ribbon of bluish airborne smoke. Paradise approached, hazily. Linda had no stretch marks. Between the wiry pad of her pubis and the buttoning of her navel was a flat satin plane. She had small breasts, too, which Konrad liked because fat was something else; he hated fat—it was too many kids, beer, peanut butter, Wonderbread, the two-car garage, the whole trip. Not Konrad. No way. But this was no time for politics, and the sitar took him to a better place in his head. Her breasts, like soft bells, clanged soundlessly and called him awake in his head. A pagoda. Konrad often had the urge to get into Eastern religion. A climbing, itching glow. Konrad closed his eyes. Linda safely solipsized, Konrad rode the hot white pulses of his own melting. Apart, there was a space between them and a space in time. Reorganized upon the sheets, she yawned and drew her panties up. Konrad cocked his arms and cradled his head from behind with his hands and smiled at the ceiling, pleased that he was different,

creative enough to have dreamed up the headphone number. But the
ceiling seemed suddenly low, and on it he allowed two faces to form.
Either/or. Beth or Linda's father, the Colonel. Parents eat the
sour grapes, said Hark, that set the children's teeth on edge. And the
Colonel, a retired warhawk in a chocolate recliner, bourbon in
hand, lost in the sound and fury of football, often set Konrad's
teeth on edge. He was a big athlete, a swimmer and skier, and he expected the family to follow; but David, her kid brother, didn't, did
grass instead, and the Yuletide turn-on possibilities kindled Konrad's interest. Besides, the Colonel, if you could get by some of
his act, wasn't all that bad. Lately he had gone soft on long hair.
And soon he was supposed to sign papers that, come Christmas,
would spring Linda's mother, June, from the jar. And the Colonel
was kind of a philosopher like himself, a mystery man of sorts, had
secrets. But one of the secrets, not so well kept, was a sun-tanned
woman from Boardman. Konrad remembered how, ice clunking in
his glass, the Colonel had lectured on the importance of a life apart,
change, the things you had to do to keep yourself alive. Konrad
knew where he was coming from and began to see that a strange
woman, like speed, might rev up his life, make more things happen.
But women couldn't hack it. Linda's mother had O.D.-ed, nearly
made the team. One weekend, Konrad had found her on the kitchen
floor. Only the dim light above the galley table, a captain's chair
overturned. On the table was a near-empty glass of water, an open
phial, one or two Yellow-jackets left. Pooled out from her white-
lipped mouth was a coagulum of bile, a cartoon bubble in which
there were no words, only small bits of pink meat. He stood and
stared at the prone form and even later, he could find no words for
his feeling. It was a heavy trip. Spaced out, Konrad regarded the
bubble in a strange way, and it seemed to be looking at him. A
scream could bring help, save her, but he couldn't scream, or must
have, because Linda jostled him, and Kiddo's eye-level mouth was
an open red flower, full of white seeds.

Day had plowed into a bleak, snowy, late afternoon. "Come
on," he urged, clapped his hands. "Let's go," he prodded, pulling

on his leather shirt with the beaded Navajo designs. "Get your coats."

"Where are we going?"

"Out. We gotta get out for a while."

Linda said she had gifts to buy.

"Good, then we can go out to the . . . ah———"

"Mall."

"Check."

Linda pursed her lips with a problem. "But I *can't* shop with"—she looked at Kiddo, then back to Konrad—"Maybe *you* could watch him while———"

"No way."

"Then what's the point of going?"

Konrad said, "What about M-i-s-s-u-s B-a-n-k-s?"

Konrad felt a light lift in himself once on the road; he liked motion. Mrs. Banks lived on the other end of Mahoning Avenue, off it actually, in a neighborhood that was slowly becoming black like his own, which was cool. They jolted slowly down a washboard street past run-down houses and pulled to a stop before a small, two-story wooden frame dwelling that was covered with tarpaper: yellow-gray bricks. In front sat a Dodge Charger on blocks; it belonged to her son who was in the army, boot camp. Kiddo began to whine, "Stay wif Mama!"

Linda said, "Go up and ask her first." Across the street, a black man got into a new Lincoln, blue, of elephantastical size. His window was down, and Konrad gave him a nod. "Hey, man."

"What's happenin?"

"Same jive."

"Right on, man," he sang in a drawn-out way and took off, his tires whining in the slush.

Being able to communicate with blacks made Konrad feel good, gave him a sense of accomplishment not unlike having learned a foreign language. He smiled to himself and climbed the wooden stairs. A green-and-white Quaker City can sat on the unpainted floor next to a rusty glider. Mrs. Banks stood by the stove, a big pot steaming. She waved him in, a tall thin woman with deep, haunted eyes and gray-black hair that was uncombed. She wore a printed house dress and black sweater with a few missing silver buttons. The room was airtight and rank with a smell of cabbage, kerosene, and sour milk that a small gray cat was lapping from a foil pie plate. There was a baby girl who sat in a cheap feeding table and had yellowish formula smeared on her mouth and chin. In the fainting warmth, Konrad asked. Yes, she would watch Kiddo. Her black eyes glowed oddly. "But remember, this is Saturday and I go to church at seven."

Konrad said he could dig it, cool, no sweat.

Car door open, Kiddo wriggled and screamed. Linda's mouth opened in sympathy, and her hand came to its rescue. It annoyed Konrad that she could not do what was necessary. Kiddo kicked, then went limp, his howl rising, choked off with repeated pleas for his mother. Kiddo clung, but Mrs. Banks pulled him loose at the door, his face red with tears. A little black boy of Kiddo's age appeared from behind her leg as Konrad backed from the foul hot rush of the kitchen, which hit him like an emetic. The black guy's kid? The little boy opened his pink mouth and laughed. Konrad looked for a moment at the two children and saw the mixed races of *Sesame Street,* and it made him feel better, even though Kiddo was still howling at the door. Mrs. Banks looked at him oddly, her eyes burning like black fire. She was . . . Konrad tried to think what she was. She wasn't bourgeois—he knew that. And that was all that mattered.

Sad smile. Silence of the sensitive for the callous. That number—he could clock her for it. They pulled on to Mahoning Avenue after what seemed like five minutes of constant carflow. Then they rolled very slowly in traffic past a mile of steel-and-glass abracadabras that sold gas, pizza, burgers, and karate with whirling gauds and parabolic yellow come-ons that lacerated the dark snowy afternoon. Konrad hit the radio and hissed. But in a moment, almost as a gift, he was given "Ventura Highway" and a good feeling came over him. Past Ho-Jo's orange roof, Konrad took the ramp and eased onto a section of interstate that would take him to

South Gate Mall. Again, the motion brought uplift and the music was mental reprieve. When the song was over, Konrad said, "We ought to cut out for Europe."

"Fine, what do we do about bread?"

"Do a little dealing."

"Cool."

"Don't you want to go to Greece?"

"Oh wow."

"What's the matter?"

"First Europe, now Greece."

"So?"

"That's where Hark is."

"So?"

Linda flicked her hair past her shoulder, gloomed out the window. "Christ, why don't you just be yourself?"

"My self's not———" He almost said *not good enough.* But it was too late; his brain had allowed the half-formed thought to pass and like a word or sign scribbled on the air, it begged to be pursued, promised gold. But Konrad let it fade, punched the radio button for a better tune. For the moment, the only gold that could promise anything was Acapulco Gold. That later.

In the thin splintering snow, Konrad perked. Something would happen. Inside, his cheekbones pulsed cold, ached with the first flash of heat. His fingers tingled. There were clowns on the first leg of the concourse. Dressed in white suits with red polka dots, they played drums and bugles and made a gathering of children laugh with slapstick routines. Linda got that sad smile again and said how it was too bad they didn't bring Kiddo.

"Stop the shit, huh?"

But Linda was going into a mood. They walked toward the sound of splashing. Konrad threw his arm around her shoulder, gave her a quick tight hug to get her up. "Hey?"

"Hey, what?"

Konrad nodded toward the fountain and asked her what it was.

"I know it's not, but let's call it a fountain."

"Wrong," said Konrad. "It's water sculpture."

"Ha, ha."

"Cool?"

"Where did you get that?"

But Konrad wouldn't say.

"You want to help me pick out a few gifts?"

"No way."

Konrad watched her shrinking toward Grant's. He could still see the sad smile. He didn't mean to say it like that; it was a phrase he liked to say, and it had to have a certain ring when you said it. That was all. Two words—they just came out. But he would not run after her to explain. No way.

Muzak with a faint holiday tune. Christ, it was the same kind of number in the jar when they went to visit June. A real down trip. On down music, down drugs, she just sat there, downed out, smiling like a moron, saying dreamy shit like "You've always . . . always . . . good girl . . . love the baby *so* much . . . hair like your. . . ." And Linda ended up crying, then annoyed him later by saying she was sorry for having cried. The memory of all those downed-out people, glassy-eyed and shuffling in slippers and green pyjamas made Konrad want to buy some hot coffee and drop a few Whites. He and the Hark never did Downs. You missed details, pissed your pants without knowing. Never would you notice a word like "Skork." Konrad hated the whole Quaalude trip that was so popular now. The fucked-up laughter and how it took a half-hour just to say "Far-out." Not for Konrad. No way.

He took his steamy black coffee to a bench next to the jungle in the middle of the concourse. There was a small waterfall, a cage of bright tropical birds that rose to the second tier of the mall. Still the dreamy muzak. People drifted along wrapped in their Saturday thoughts. Drifted. Konrad felt himself drifting, losing the lift he had a while ago, the good sense of being alone, of something about to happen. Last year, on one of these bleak Youngstown afternoons, he saw two girls fighting and tearing each other's clothing in the service alley. High, Konrad had sat exactly where he was now. Some high school guys laughed and cheered, "Go Torpedo" and "Fire

One." One girl bled from the nose onto her white torn blouse. It was a funny scene, had lots of color.

But now nothing. Konrad stared at the coated figures on the escalator and felt himself taken by the trancelike way they ascended with muzak, gripping the black rubber rails, standing in different attitudes, but all disappearing, one by one, willy-nilly. Christ! And turning, he spooked at his image in plate glass; it was a shoe store. He came closer, a diver in an aquarium. Hanging nets. Fake doubloons in the sand, in the expensive shoes. A phony treasure chest. Tropical fish made out of bright paper dangled and twisted on white threads. The scene was somehow teasingly familiar, depressing. Konrad looked away at the droves of people on the concourse. All hungry for the same bourgeois bait, all buying costumes for the same look-alike trip. He had to get his act together, make some kind of scene. This was a downer, very unhip. And the lulling muzak. But he could move; he could always do that; he did.

Near the exit was a Little Professor Bookstore with a trademark symbol above the entrance: an orange moon wearing a black mortarboard and tassel, absurdly small; and, in the middle of the eyeless, noseless, and mouthless face, an owlish pince-nez. The whole number put Konrad in mind of Beth's husband, the bookman. A New Year's party not enough years ago. Other moony faces were there. Drinks atop hand-held elbows; bodies swaying like channel buoys. "Then tell us, Konrad, how would you define it?" *Define.* Oh wow. Like David Frost always asking what, in fact, is your definition of love? An ice cube clunked in the short quiet. A giggle nearby. The moony faces, waiting. But Konrad couldn't define it, mumbled that bourgeois something was an ego-trip, the whole number. And before someone else spoke, there came snickers to his ears. Snickers, he was sure of it. So he moved between phantom people toward the door, then out.

It had stopped snowing. In the cold car, Konrad pulled out the seat molding, teased out a small bag of grass, and felt a sweet quickening; it was the Illegal, a turn-on by itself. Danger. Like when he used to get it off with Linda when her father was in the next room watching TV. Konrad could still see that thick sculpted carpet: all those rivers, countries, continents, and islands. But there had been giggles, snickers. A red Olds pulled into the diagonal slot just opposite. A guy with an Astrakhan hat got out of his car and fumbled about with his key, finally locking it. Konrad laughed. He could open it faster with a coat hanger. The guy had a cocky walk, probably thought he was the coolest item in town with that hat. Konrad had the urge to kick his ass. But the man was gone, and Konrad had better things to do. He sprinkled, rolled, and licked. Then he pulled out the molding again and tamped the bag back into place. He finally lit up, took three deep tokes, and began, it seemed, to feel already that delicious helium lift, a warm cloud expanding in his chest. The neon SEARS pulsed greenly, nicely. He flipped on the radio; he needed that too. Snickers were coming again and the fatback guitar held them at bay; it was "Long Train Runnin'," and Konrad did a little tattoo on the wheel, nodded his head. Toke and swallow, hold. He gazed at the lovely SEARS through a luminous feeling, like a milky swamp gas. Then it was "A Whole Lotta Love," an oldie and one of the Hark's favorites. The radio had a beautiful orange face. A big truck went by; it said 7UP THE UN-COLA.

Linda got in. She didn't smile. "Cool" was all she said. Folded her arms. What was this act? She used to dig his unpredictability. Once, before they were married, she said it was his novelty she loved. He was exciting to be around. Unexpected joint smoke used to fetch a giggle. But not like the party giggle, the snicker. Linda hadn't the faintest trace of a smile. There was a gray moue at the mouth, pain lines at the eyes. But what the fuck was this?

"It's almost seven."

"So?"

"Mrs. Banks, remember?"

"Be cool." Konrad unslouched.

"Be cool," she mocked.

He snicked on the ignition. The keys hung twisting and untwisting; they ticked against and chafed the column. A red oil light glowed. Konrad headed for the south exit and in an empty section of the huge parking lot, he deliberately fishtailed the car. He laughed. Linda sucked in her breath. "Please," she said. She touched his arm. But Konrad was oblivious. Under the red light, Linda's face was red, rigid. Wasn't he being creative enough? A rat-cornered fear ran through him. Linda knew his act. He changed it daily, but it was the same. So what? He could impress others. And maybe would. Time maybe for the Colonel's act. Still, he felt naked, hit the volume, dressed himself in a Dylan lyric. "How-does-it-fee-yul?" he sang, then let Dylan take it. " . . . no dir-ect-shun home . . . like-a-com-plete un-known . . . like-a-roll-in stone. . . . "

When the light changed, Konrad goosed it and felt a sleek thrill when the rear end of the car began to pass him on the right. Linda bit her lip. Konrad laughed and hung a left.

"Where are we going?"

"We've never been this way before."

Linda was mute. Konrad expected static but none came; he was disappointed. There was no way for him to say *no way*. The road rivered whitely away, and the car drifted smoothly. Konrad tried to get her up, himself up. "Come on! What the hell. Give Kiddo a little Jesus trip." But Linda didn't laugh. Dylan whined nasally: "How-does-it-fee-yul?" Again and again. Konrad caught side glimpses of Linda. It was farmland all around, and she was ruining it, ruining the nice guitar, the rising harmonica wail, the indigo sky, and huge country stars. Christ, what was she into? Her cheeks were polished with tears. He felt some huge presence out ahead of the car; it was looking in, taking stock of his act, disapproving, saying no. The small lift of motion unlifted. The tall handsome roadside dark, which only a moment ago spun with adventure, unspun. Konrad's hand's trembled. He mumbled magic formulae: "Hey, get your head together . . . coming from with this uptight jive . . . no way . . . I thought I knew where your head was at . . . now this bummer . . . heavy into this Hollywood number. . . . " Linda keened. The tumble of words did not want to stop. Konrad was frightened. He wasn't choosing words; they were choosing him, like fleas a dog, until he heard the word "bourgeois" spat at Linda. But as he looked at her crying, sobbing violently, her thin shoulders shaking, he knew that wasn't it. It was. . . . He tried to think. Dylan taunted, "How-does-it-fee-yul?" Konrad sent out his hand to the volume, and the song disappeared with a click. He took his foot off the gas. The car slowed. His head ached. He tried to think; he tried to think what it was.

Breaking and Entering

Harold was surprised.

He was surprised that the front door gave without a key, was surprised at his reaction: he sprang back to the car and told his wife, Nance, removing shopping bags from the trunk, to run to the Revards' and call the cops. "Why?" she complained, and he hissed, "Goddammit, do it!" And spun her around.

Harold snatched a jack handle from the trunk; it felt almost hot, alive in his hand. Tomorrow, alone, he would wonder at his reaction—was it the film he had just seen?—because, as the house loomed blackly above him, he began to experience a sense of abandonment. He had no shotgun, no partner to cut off escape, but here already was the door banging against the inside wall, Harold in the hallway, coiled and waiting with the huge sound of his heart. No tipped-over chairs, scattered cushions, emptied drawers, tilted pictures, as he had somehow imagined. But there were painful gaps. A blank space against the wall where the color TV had been, empty shelves in place of the Pioneer amp and records. An obscene emptiness. "Son-of-a-bitch," he rasped, announcing his presence at the same time. But there was no answering sound from the rest of the house. It was hot and airless and his face flushed with anger, shame. The heavy weight of the jack handle tugged at his arm; he looked at it and instantly wished he had instructed Nance differently.

In the kitchen the broiler oven was gone. Things were brutally out of sync with memory, like the tongue, incredulous, returning and lingering where teeth used to be, or gently exploring the leaky cracks of a swollen lip. *Punky said you said he was queer. He wants to see you outside. You better suck on that Coke, man, real slow.* It was a flash from high school. Vince always rode shotgun in Punky's deuce coupe. Punky was waiting in the parking lot outside Friendly's, where they hung around at night and after football games. Harold could feel his stomach awash with fear, taste its brass in his mouth. *You callin' Vince here a liar? Hunh, Harold?*

"Harold?"

"Harry?" The second voice belonged to Revard. "Harry, you okay?" Revard had a .38 snubnose, cocked, pointed toward the ceiling, as he flattened himself against the wall the way detectives did in the movies. "You check upstairs, Harry?"

Depressed that he even knew Revard, who had a praying mantis face and would never have been in the high school gang, Harold nodded. Revard sold wire to hardware stores, had a past that couldn't quite be nailed down, but let on that he knew where the action was, could get you stuff at half-price, stuff that had accidentally (wink) fallen off the back of a truck. He had stories about himself that were laughable. "You sure, Harry? Sombitch might still be upstairs."

"I'm sure," snapped Harold. "I'm sure."

Nance's mouth fell open; she looked aghast, and made a move to lean on the counter. Revard moved quickly, grabbing her arm. "Nance, you'll wipe off the prints."

She sank to a chair. "Blender, TV, broiler oven. . . . "

Harold left them and went upstairs. An odd smell uncurled on the hot air. In the spare room something was missing—what? The Singer portable, a birthday gift. And the electric typewriter: there was a dark dustless square on the desktop. Backing from the room, Harold felt an old tension in his stomach and limbs, as before a basketball game, or a parking lot rumble. But what was that smell? He snapped on the bedroom light, and his eyes focused on the open bureau drawer where Nance kept her jewelry, what little she had. But it was gone, rosewood box and all. Gone. And replaced with a smell that, as he turned, revealed its source on the bed—a small glossy, dark pile on the nubby white spread, two brownish smears

near the tasseled corner. Harold looked away and caught himself in
the bureau mirror retreating, a lean face with shiny black eyes and
thick brows, a big jaw, the mouth struggling with horror and rage.

He closed the bedroom door, took a deep breath, and stepped
into the upstairs hall, which pulsed with red light from the window
at the foot of the stairwell. Voices buzzed in confusion. A policeman
met Harold at the bottom of the stairs, a burly man his own age but
with a serrated growl for a voice. He introduced himself as Sergeant
Davis. Harold could see him grunting and sweating in a handball pit
at the YMCA. "What've we got upstairs?"

But Harold hesitated; he was distracted by another policeman
entering the front room, holding a huge silver flashlight with red
sheathing around the lens; he was looking at Harold intently.
"Look, ah ——— "

Harold gave his name.

"Look, Harold, what's the matter up there?" asked Davis.

Harold told him that jewelry and a sewing machine were gone.

"Let's have a look."

But Harold remained on the stairs, blocking the way. Davis
looked at him suspiciously now. "Look, Harold, what's the
matter?" Reluctantly he stepped aside, and the policeman went up
the carpeted stairs.

Forcing a smile, Nance said: "Our insurance will cover."

"Sure," said Harold, knowing it would never cover how he felt.

Revard, eyes glittering, asked: "What they get upstairs?" His
pistol was tucked away. He looked at Harold, tapped his belt, and
winked. Harold felt like driving his fist into Revard's insect face. He
noticed a crowd of neighbors in the drive by the squad cars, which
pulsed redly in the June heat. He knew none of them, though he had
lived here for more than a year. And he wished he had never met
Revard. "Do you mind," he told the other policeman, "telling
those morons to beat it." The cop told him to cool it. Nance agreed
and said he should take it easy. "People are just curious," she said
and touched his arm, which recoiled as if from something vile.

"They're enjoying it."

Pleadingly she whispered his name.

He couldn't bring himself to tell her about upstairs.

"Well, well," said Davis in that loud growl of his, "a rip-off artist who's a little on the sick side."

Nance flashed a question mark. The other policeman looked at Harold. Harold said, "He left a pile of feces on our bed."

In the soft earth under the windows, behind the shrubs, they looked for footprints. The flashlight beam slid around the lawn. A hot black wall of trees secluded the house on three sides. Crickets were strident, constant, like those fucking voices that carried into the back yard. "Where does that path go?" graveled Davis.

"A short cut to the high school." Harold felt the other cop watching him in the dark. They knew each other from somewhere. Maybe the Lounge Bar. The guy was dark and puffy, with a long bony nose and deep eyepits. He startled Harold by asking if the path didn't also come out on Rosemary Street.

"That's right," said Harold. "A new street, only a few houses." Davis said: "Ten to one that's where he parked the truck. We'll check it out, maybe get some tire tracks."

Back in the house, the bony-nosed cop said: "Beautiful yard, lots of privacy—just the kind of thing a burglar loves."

Harold glanced at the nameplate above his pocket; it said, in white-on-black, JOSEPH TERNOVA. There seemed a faint leer on his face. "He's right," growled Davis. "You should have a light back there." TERNOVA. Harold wondered. An old face from Friendly's? Maybe he was from up the valley, Watertown. A member of the Diabolos. Lots of Italians. Harold's gang had had a running battle with them.

Nance sat at the kitchen table. Revard was still hanging around; watching, listening, he leaned against the doorjamb.

"Look," said Davis hoarsely, "I want you to make a complete list of what's gone. We'll pick it up tomorrow. Give the serial numbers and ——— "

"Serial numbers?" asked Nance.

"That's right, ma'am. For purposes of identification."

Ternova stopped chewing his gum and sighed. "We try an' educate the public, but nobody listens.'' He shook his head. ''Last week the *Chronicle* ran a piece about our engraver. You read it?''

Nance said no.

The policemen looked at each other. Davis's eyeballs rolled, as if they were tracking a fly on the ceiling—ah, the futility of it all! Ternova removed his hat and dragged a black hairy forearm across his sweaty brow. With the tool, which was loaned freely, explained Ternova, you could engrave your name on the metal chassis of a TV, say, so that it would be easily identified as a hot item, therefore difficult to fence and easy for police to use in prosecuting a case. With ragged nerves Harold listened to talk that had little to do with how he felt. His face was broiling. Every missing item was a taunt, the step beyond a threat: defeat. And these two uniforms were making it worse, were asking—what? If Harold and Nance did the same thing every Friday night? Nance was answering before he could say a thing.

''Well, I guess.'' It was really none of their business, but here she was confessing to these cops that, yes, on Friday they generally came home from work, had a drink and cleaned up, went shopping at the mall, had dinner in the Chinese or Mexican restaurant, took in a film, and got home around midnight.

Joseph Ternova repeated the question, almost with leering pleasure it seemed to Harold. ''So, in other words, you do the same thing *every Friday*?''

''No, not the same thing,'' Harold put in.

''But,'' boomed Davis, ''you're away from the house for a pre-dict-able period of time.''

''Right,'' said Nance.

Harold inhaled. His shirt was soaked. He had to say it: ''We don't do exactly the same thing.''

Ternova said: ''Friday evenings you're not here, right?''

Nance frowned.

Harold hesitated.

Ternova noted something in his pad, then, with fatuous finality, said: ''Same difference.''

''See,'' clarified Davis, ''your be-havior is pre-dict-able. Anybody watching you for a few days could know when to hit. By the way, you noticed anybody strange, any strange cars on the street?''

That Harold didn't shamed him; he used to be sharp-eyed. And the newspapers had been recently full of the story of how Jock Yablonski, the murdered UMW official, had in effect delivered his own murderers by having written down their license numbers as they cased his home; he then put the numbers in his safe where they were found by investigators in the bloody aftermath. It was chilling. Harold often wondered what he would do if his house were broken into while he was there. The thought, in fact, occurred to him just before Revard left. On the sly Revard whispered, ''You, ah''—tapped his pocket—''you wanna borrow my piece?''

Harold wished he hadn't hesitated before saying no.

''Sure? I still got my .357.''

Firmly Harold said no.

The latent-prints man, in street clothes with a police I.D. clipped to the pocket of his green shirt, finished dusting and brushing knobs, handles, bannisters, switch-plates, and other likely surfaces. He also inked *their* fingerpads and rolled prints onto cards with spaces for each digit and palm. It made Harold feel as if he were somehow guilty. And the officers—they had found an unlocked rear window—didn't do anything to alter Harold's guilt and the feeling he had brought this all on himself. They shook their heads in unison, a gesture meant to express the sad naiveté of most people. *Do you do the same thing every Friday?* Harold saw smears on the white bedspread, and screams wanted to shoot off within him, but Ternova, on the porch, was asking him if he had any enemies. Harold tried to think. The black-and-white cruiser in the drive, still pulsing red light, silver badges floating in the dark, two alien faces full of shadow—Harold saw everything with the feeling he was not where he was, that this was not really his house.

''Well, think on it,'' said Ternova.

''We'll keep an eye on the house.''

''No real need to worry.''

Harold was incredulous. Were they trying to scare him? Having a little fun? *Punky's a tough muvva, man. Beat the livin' shit outta*

Mista Pinch afta school. "Worry about what?" asked Harold.
"Why would he come back?"

The cops looked at each other, shrugged. "Look, ah, Harold,
we'll be in touch."

Crickets jeered. Harold looked from one face to the other. The
eyes hid under the shiny black peaks of their hats. "I'll tell you one
thing," he heard himself saying, as if from a distance. "If that creep
comes back, he'll be one sorry sonofabitch!"

In the hot foul air Harold watched the police car swing onto the high
road at the end of the street. Upstairs the toilet flushed. Nance came
down carrying the soiled bedclothes and mattress pad in a ball. In
the utility room, with the top of the washing machine up, she paused
and looked at him. A wrinkle came to her forehead; the look
prodded him: "So why did you laugh when I said *feces*?"

She laughed again. "It struck me funny."

He watched her reach into the machine, her tan thighs tighten as
she rose on her toes. Vulnerable. She had lovely limbs and a graceful
neck, blond hair, and lute-shaped eyes. She laughed quickly and
easily, her reactions were quirky, and she gave the impression of being flighty; but control and solidity were her strong points. A few
years ago, when his father died and he had gone berserk with grief
and drink, she confidently coaxed him out of a trite bar and back to
life. He felt foolish. "Funny how?"

"You know, you're usually more scatological."

She was being kind: he was vulgar and he knew it. Her swing into
education had produced results; his master's degree, he often
thought, was a joke. The degree meant no social or financial advance and, more important, he knew he was unchanged as a person:
he was still coarse and it cost him an effort to refrain from foul
language.

In the bedroom he looked out of the window; the wall of trees was
insultingly black. "But laughing at a time like that, in front of
those ——— "

She turned. "What am I supposed to do, *cry*? That would be
easy."

Harold shook his head. "You're not angry?"

"You're taking this personally and"—she almost laughed—
"there's nobody to aim your anger at. Even if they catch somebody. . . . "

"*Catch somebody*—are you kidding? Those fingerprints have
already been filed and forgotten!"

"I'm saying"—she raised her voice—"I'm saying that it was im-
personal. The guy didn't even know us. Anger needs an object. . . . "

But Harold did have an object: Ternova. And Pape, a workmate,
one of the subs at the P.O. Pape was skinny, oily, and had long fretful hands. He was always standing before his sorting rack with a
girlie magazine, and the guys ragged him if he spent more than a
minute in the men's room. But Pape's face changed places with Ternova's and others, became a montage of anonymous laughing
mouths cropped with teeth until only Nance remained looking at
him calmly. The calmness itself was a taunt.

"I don't understand you," she said, and sat down on the bed
where it had been soiled and began removing her shoes.

"That makes two of us," said Harold. "Look, you don't know
those cops, that mentality. You give those guys no more than necessary. They don't have to know about our Fridays or anything else.
They—wait, let me finish. I know those guys. In high school they
wore gang jackets and engineer boots. They're punks. Nothing they
like better than to have an edge on you."

Hangers clinked in the closet. Harold had a glimpse of Ternova in
a Diabolo jacket. The Watertown Diabolos. A dead-end street and a
dozen guys fighting. . . .

"People change, Harold." She was in her nightie and getting into
bed. Always generous. She possessed a goodness and had an above-
life quality that maddened him. It was uncanny; only a few hours
ago some creep had lowered his trousers here, and she could say she
was tired and actually get into that bed as if nothing had happened.
"It's nearly three o'clock," she said. "Tomorrow it'll be the insurance man and everything. You had better come to bed."

"I can't."

"Try. Make yourself a drink." She settled her head into the

pillow. Harold smelled—perhaps he imagined it—a fecal odor lingering in the room. "You'll feel better in the morning," she said.

But it *was* morning, and sleep wouldn't come. With a beer in hand he sat and gazed at the blank space where the TV used to be. A kind of mockery surfaced everywhere an item was missing. Worse than mockery, each object gone was felt as a bruise. It must be something like rape, he thought. *Punky wants to see you outside.* Nothing could be quite the same any more; he felt like moving. *You do the same thing every Friday?* No. He had never sat alone drinking beer without the lighted face of the TV to hold his consciousness. Everything felt strange, unfamiliar, tainted. He lay on the sofa. It was impossible to sleep upstairs with Nance. He had to be alone.

On the edge of sleep, near dawn, he was jerked back: a cracking stick in the woods, movement in the dead leaves. His heart struggled. He grabbed the jack handle and flashlight he had earlier placed between his legs. The beer can fell from its balance on his chest and clanked softly on the carpet. On the back porch he listened. Leaves crackled near the Sears utility shed. The guy was still in the woods, just behind the stone wall, thought Harold, and hit the light. Two eyes shone back like a pair of hellish red taillights. He angled the light for a better look and saw a raccoon, the hump back and the bandit mask of a second-story man. Harold made a hissing sound, but it wouldn't scare, and only a flung rock finally sent it on a switchback run through the trees.

In the living room he stood by the window. There was a haze of sweat in the air. You could see it under the light where the street deadended. There was a bat, which dove and swerved, slicing the air into pieces of a black design. *The taillights of the other car lit in a red panic at the dead end. Six guys from Watertown in a '51 Buick with primer spots. The kid riding shotgun spat a big hawker on Harold's front fender and was going to get his. Sykes blocked the rest of the street with his Olds. Four guys in his car too. Eight to six: nice odds. And in engineer boots and club jackets they piled out and began drawing blood with chains, heavy-buckled belts, and knuckles. Harold got the spitter with a jack handle; one swing and the kid was out. And another kid with a long bony nose caught Harold on the ear, and they were going at it when a porch light went on and an old guy in a bathrobe began yelling about the cops. A siren howled in the distance, and they began to take off. But the spitter from Watertown just lay there bleeding, his head turned in a funny way. He wasn't even moving, but Sykes gave him another boot, and Harold had to pull him off.*

When he stepped from the shower, he could hear Nance; her voice was animated, and she was telling her friend Patty about the burglary. He didn't know whether it was the start of the story or the finish or how much had been told. But nothing should be told and the expression on his face must have said as much. "I've got to go," said Nance. "Talk to you later."

"Yeah, later," said Harold.

"Why? What's the matter?"

"Why does everyone have to know our business?"

"Patty's not everyone."

"I'm sorry."

"Patty is no blabbermouth and you know it."

"Christ, I said I'm sorry." Something sickening had happened to them, and the only consolation was that it gave them a story—a story that for a few days made them unique. But Harold was against being unique in that way.

"What will we say to our parents on Friday?"

Harold saw Ternova's leering face. *You do the same thing every Friday night?* He called Saner, the superintendent of mails, and said something urgent came up and he wouldn't be in until later in the afternoon. But that brought no relief. Cicadas were screaming in the woods, and the green yard colors were already flattened by the sun. A small transistor radio sat on the counter and gibbered with its tin voice: "Increased prices . . . major oil companies . . . added costs passed on to consumers. . . . "

The insurance man wore a light-colored suit, plum shirt, and smoke-tinted glasses, was losing his hair, but appeared, Harold thought, no older than himself. The guy was standardized swank, trying to make it as elegant. A uniform really. And when he began, beaming with pride, to tout his company, talk deductibles and quick settlements, Harold found it difficult to keep his hands still. "I have a pamphlet you should study closely . . . tips for protecting your home . . . shrubs . . . beautiful but perfect cover . . . privacy and protection at odds . . . burglaries up 23% . . . more than three million last year alone. . . ."

Harold stood up abruptly and left the room. The guy somehow reminded him of Holmes, a strident high school thespian, a kid who also ran the projector in civics. When he left, Harold said, "I was bad, hunh?"

"Don't expect me to disagree."

"But I just can't *deal* with guys like that."

"Maybe if you'd deal with yourself. . . . " She said it in a tone of exasperation.

Harold watched her leave the room; he wondered how she would deal with the things he had had to deal with. He wondered. He had never seen her lose control.

A white Ford with big blue letters saying CRIME PREVENTION pulled into the drive. The chrome dazzled. Harold watched a small man—a man with black hair that touched the ears, mirror sunglasses, and a swaggering bowlegged walk, long bony nose. Ternova. In daylight he looked different. Harold decided to talk to him on the porch, in the sun. Nance, through the screen, suggested Harold invite the officer in. Ternova said, "Thanks anyway, ma'am, I'm just going to be a minute. It's been a long shift."

Harold gave him the list of missing things that Nance had written up. Ternova rested one hand on his holster; the leather creaked. Harold thought of a saddle, a horse, of a high school math teacher they used to torment by nickering, tossing their heads, hoofing out answers on the floor because the man had a long equine face and big front teeth. In high school Harold used to size up guys in his classes, decide whether or not he could take them—not an idle activity, for the boys' rooms, hallways, and parking lots were full of no-exit situations. Harold felt none of the current nostalgia for the fifties, in fact hated those years, and suddenly felt shame to discover himself sizing up Ternova in that old crazy prefight way.

"Think you'll get the guy?"

"Why not *guys*?" asked Ternova.

"Okay, plural."

"Policework ain't like TV, you know. It's part luck too. Sometimes you have to wait for 'em to make a mistake." Then, as an afterthought: "Or *plural* mistakes." He smirked and surveyed the yard. He snapped the clipboard and looked at Harold, who saw himself distorted in the mirror sunglasses, squinting, exasperation magnified. Ternova leaned against the porch railing and looked at the sky. "Did you, ah, used to live in Clifton?"

Harold said yes.

"Go to Central High?"

Harold said yes.

"Didn't used to drive, ah"—he grinned faintly as if zeroing in—"a 53 burnt-orange Merc?"

Harold was sure. Ternova had been there that night the spitter's skull had been fractured. Harold could see Ternova's lean teenage face under the one padded with cop-fat. They had gone at it before the porch light went on and everyone scattered at the sound of the siren.

"No," Harold lied. He made himself laugh.

"Nosed and decked?"

"Hell no. *Burnt orange!* I've got better taste than that."

"Sure, sure, I must be wrong," he said, meaning he sure as hell wasn't. But changed the subject. "Where you say you work?" He stepped off the porch.

"Post office."

"Post office, hunh?" He stood beside the CRIME PREVENTION car. "You like it?"

"Yeah, why not?"

Ternova sniffed. "It's, ah, kind of—*routine,* isn't it?"

Ternova was asking for it. Harold had an urge to dice him verbally but somehow didn't. "Look, anything can be routine. I've got an old college buddy who flies for TWA, 747s; he's bored stiff, says it's a pain in the ass." Harold was mildly pleased with his show of reason.

But Ternova said, "*College* buddy, hunh?" He paused. "Hey, I almost forgot." He fished in his shirt pocket. "How about helping us out?"

"How?"

Ternova handed him two blue tickets. "PBA picnic."

Harold wished he hadn't accepted the tickets; returning them would be like *shove* responding to *push*—something he hoped he had outgrown.

"Hey, it's only two bucks apiece. For the kids. Keep 'em off the street, keep 'em from riding around in cars looking for fights with guys from the next town." His mouth wore a crooked smile. "You won't regret it." His tone was ironic.

To color things, Harold said, handing him four limp bills: "Hey, where's my receipt?"

"Don't worry, the tickets are numbered." He started the engine. "Besides I'm a honest injun." He grinned and slipped it into reverse. "Happy trails," he said, and backed into the street, engulfing himself and disappearing in his cloud of dust.

Hell. Harold stood in the head-pounding sun, sweating, half-seeing the CRIME PREVENTION car, through its own wake of dust and exhaust, swing onto the high road at the end of the street. He hated to lose and *loser* was the only word that pulsed in his head. PBA tickets, meaning: *if you don't buy, we may not be able to. . . .* And Ternova was probably laughing to himself at that moment—the moment Nance met him at the door, her face animated, and said she didn't have to be to work at the library until four o'clock. She winked, but the signal didn't register. Harold was elsewhere. She put her arm around him. Maybe he would relax if they took a little (sly smile) nap. He was puzzled by her animation, her carefree mood—or was it feigned? She seemed—it was probably his fatigue and anger and bewilderment—but she seemed almost quickened by this whole thing. On the wall was a dark square of green where the TV had kept the paint from fading.

"Are you all right?"

"Sure I'm all right."

"Then why are you shrugging me off?"
"I'm not. I've just got to get out. I'm going to work."
"You haven't eaten."
"I'll have lunch at the diner for a change."

Raking the big room from atop the sorting racks, three fans created currents of dead hot air that gave no relief. And loud rock music was constant from an unseen radio in another aisle. Whitey, one of the old guys, a retired navy man, said the radio got on his nerves, but somebody else said, "I don't hear anything, do you, Brud?"

"Nah," said Brud, "I don't hear a thing."

" 'Cause that stuff's made ya deaf as a pecker!" yelled Whitey.

"You old bastard, give us young guys a break."

Harold stood near the time clock; he knew they weren't finished with Whitey. The technique for torment involved repetition and variation. Soon somebody would say: *Hey, that's a great tune, turn it up a little.* Whitey, pushed to a boil, would be abandoned for a time, and attention would shift to Pape, another figure of fun. It was too familiar; it was like high school. Even college. No fighter, Pape was like Elmo, a guy who lived in the room next to Harold in college. Elmo was skinny too and the brunt of every prank in the book.

Harold clocked in. He could see every missing item in the house, feel every empty space like a burn. He thought of Pape, Elmo. It was awful: the fountain, bulletin board, empty parcel hampers, pigeonholed racks—they seemed to have just stopped laughing. There was a lull in the usual din. The radio crackled news about oil companies: "Consumers absorb . . . costs will be passed on. . . . " Passed on—the words echoed in his head. Then a broken chain of cackles and coarse laughs came from the coffee room. Harold heard a voice say, "Pape, he really stuck it to ya."

"Put the boots to ya, I'd say."

"Roasted," sang another voice.

Cackles and hoots.

"Hey, Pape!"

"Pape, you gonna take that?"

God. The afternoon, Harold knew, would drone on in needling

variations. But he would stay out of it—he had for more than a year. Pape had tried to stay out of it too, but they found him. They always found people like Pape. Like Elmo. *Bly had carded Elmo's door and had it open. Harold felt himself grinning foolishly and having to say, "Okay, men, let's get to work." Bly and Nims laughed and with gleeful squeals began carrying off things in Elmo's room. "Hi ho, hi ho, it's off to work we go," they sang. Bly said, "He'll love it." And Elmo so thoroughly accepted his clown/victim role it was hard to think otherwise. Harold and Bly lugged the desk down the hall and put it in the last shower stall. Everyone took something from the room and hid it until even the bed was gone—removed via the firestairs and placed next to a spinning ventilator on the roof. The room was totally bare, the wall eerily blank, naked of its warming posters. Bly's fat round face was gashed with cackles. "I can't wait"—he shook with spasms of laughter—"to see the . . . look . . . on that . . . foolish face of his." Someone else said, "This'll be even better than the time we handcuffed him to the radiator!" A voice at the end of the hall said, "I think he's coming." Everyone scurried to separate rooms, but it was a false alarm. All afternoon and evening they hung around and waited for him to return from Boston. "Son-of-a-bitch is spoiling our fun." Everyone laughed. Nims said, "Maybe he's shacking up with his girl." Bly said, "What's a looker like her doing with foolish Elmo?" Nims said, "Maybe the secret's in his underwear!" But it wasn't a good laugh. They had waited too long, and when Elmo returned from Boston near midnight, nobody laughed. He went berserk, howled in misery; great cries of anguish exploded from the horribly empty room. With each cry Harold bounced in his bunk, as if shocked electrically. Even with the pillow clasped to his burning ears, he could hear Elmo shrieking, "I'm a jerk, I'm a jerk," over and over as he banged his head against the wall until Father Anthony came to take him to the infirmary for a sedative.*

"Pape, you jerko."

"Pape, I wouldn't take that."

Harold stared at his bench; it was a chaos of deliberately heaped and strewn Second, Third, and Fourth Class. More than a dozen pieces had fallen to the floor; it was a kind of message: *I may have had to walk your lousy dog-infested route, but I sure as hell ain't throwing it.* But from whom? Harold got to his knees, retrieved the fallen pieces; he stood up, began sorting, and it clicked: Pape. Sure, Pape was appointed to take his route. The taunts about getting stuck. Well, well. Poor Pape. That took guts, even though they egged him into it. And now he heard another theme, in a thin piping voice: "Mama Bear, *somebody* shit in my bed!"

Then a deep voice: "Nobody shit in *my* bed."

"Anybody shit in *your* bed?"

Hot cackles and hoots rang in his ears. The voice was coming from behind a rack near the parcel hampers; it belonged to Big Dick Howard. All the guys said you had to dick him before he dicked you. A face with no harmony: little eyes, rutabaga nose, delicate lips, and curly hair slapped on as an afterthought. Fish-belly skin. Harold didn't even remember the shot that finally knocked Howard into the canvas parcel-hamper. Feet above his head, Howard struggled on his back like a turtle. "Did *you* shit in my bed?" screamed Harold. "Hunh?" And he cracked him in the mouth. "Hunh?" And he cracked him again.

But now the guys hustled him through the swinging doors onto the loading dock. Howard staggered after and grabbed onto one of the metal canopy supports; a channel of bright blood ran from the corner of his puffed eye; the mouth seemed smeared with cherry pie. "I'll kill you, you wait. I swear I'll kill you," he yelled, but he made no attempt to follow Harold across the street and through the baseball field toward the woods. The super, Saner, was yelling too, yelling that Harold had forgotten to clock out.

The light was violent and thumped him on the head, and the advancing trees were out of focus, as if from a blow. There was no air, and his heart-pounding pace wouldn't slow, and he wondered if he would make the shade or pass out. Though not old, he kept thinking *heart attack, heart attack.* But the knocking against his sternum grew less as he leaned on a wild cherry with black scaly bark. The dappled green began to calm him. Harold took deep breaths and began walking again. Bird-sound caught his attention, and he tried to distinguish the birds becoming momentarily brilliant as they darted through pools of sunlight and winged themselves to hidden perches: bluejay, catbird, thrasher. He had to work his mind. Christ, it was unbearable; his cheeks burned. University, master's, years of school, music, art, and philosophy for this. He looked at his battered knuckles, blood drying to a color of rust. Jesus. But the joke was malicious and he would not be made a figure of fun. The CRIME PREVENTION car—he thought he remembered seeing it in the distance, as he walked to work, pull away from the front steps of the post office. Ternova was tight with one of the carriers. Sure. Because the *Chronicle* was off the press at two o'clock, but the Police Notes would have said nothing about the soiled bed. It had to have been a detail provided by Ternova. The name echoed in his head: over, over. But was it? High school again. Instead of absorbing and quietly dissipating his anger, he passed it on. And there was no honor in that. High school— maybe it went on forever and you learned to live with it, like this hot foul air.

He came to the railroad tracks and crossed them and entered another woods that was contiguous with the back of his property. Above a small pond bordered by a thin stand of reeds, gnats were tossing in a loose bottle like angry bits of advancing dark. Harold followed the path along the old stone wall that ran to his back yard. He couldn't go home like this. He'd wait. Nance would be leaving for the library soon. On the wooded knoll just above the house, he sat down and leaned against a great lichened boulder. At the corner of the house the white clapboard had a stain, a reddish runnel creeping downward and widening. It was gutter rust and looked awful. Nance had told him about it and wanted it fixed. Part of him wanted to tell her what happened. But what would he say? *Ever since last night—I don't know why—I've had these flashes about high school and college and some things we did. One is about that cop, Ternova, and a gang fight we were both in as high school kids. The other is about a guy, an out-of-it guy in my dorm we used to torment. But in this gang fight we almost killed a guy. I hit him with a jack handle, and he went down like an axed pig. Just his muscles twitched. Then Sykes kicked him, and he went still as a stone. I thought we killed him. I was terrified. Every night I read the papers to see if the guy died. But we ——*

He stopped himself. We, we—a lie. Harold was too tired to lie.
And the *confiteor* would turn theatrical. But Nance would have a
book splayed in her lap, her expression sympathetic, understanding.
He thought of his father, what he had once said: *You may be sorry,
Harold, but that changes nothing.* Nance, though, would say it all
happened a long time ago and everyone sooner or later experiences
remorse—late at night or on rainy days. It was normal. But Harold
wasn't sure he wanted to be normal. And his contrition might be
false because last night again that jack handle had given him the
kind of intense feeling he hadn't experienced in years. But that rush
and tingle had gone, and now he felt very tired, his limbs heavy. He
leaned back against the rock and listened to sounds—a faraway car-
horn, the nearby morse of a woodpecker—and waited for Nance to
leave for the library.

You may be sorry, Harold, but that changes nothing. He tried to
control his breathing and breathed through his nose the sweetness of
lilac that drifted up from the side yard in slow eddies. Harold
wanted to believe somebody who said that where there was sorrow,
there was holy ground. But he didn't know, couldn't feel it exactly.
Then, yes. He realized it wasn't so much the high school rumble,
bad as it was, that made him feel as he did—it was Elmo, poor
Elmo. It was the breaking and entering. That was it. And suddenly
he felt himself possessed by a great sorrow and a longing to reach
Elmo wherever he was, apologize, and hear Elmo say it was all right.
But all he could hear was that horrible bonking within his head and
the indelible refrain: *I'm a jerk, jerk, jerk.* . . .

Harold shuddered, breathed deeply, and got to his feet. He had
been sitting for a long time, and his head swam. He had to lean
against the boulder. "O God," he moaned. His shoulders ached. It
was almost dark again. Nance was gone and the house empty. TV
gone. He didn't know if he could enter the house, but he felt he had
to. The reddish stain on the white clapboard grew as he stepped
from the woods onto the lawn. He advanced, choosing each step
deliberately.

Big in Osaka

The side of the coach was stainless steel; it was polished and so clean I would have seen myself perfectly except for the horizontal fluting. The end of a pleasant two-day trip. Amtrak was clean, smooth, air-conditioned—a world better than the slow, filthy, hot coaches I rode years ago as a student. I'd probably say something like that to Latch, whom I was meeting in a bar around the corner from the station. At the right time I'd say I was sorry his father had died.

It was certain my father wouldn't be there, but I still ran my eyes over the platform. He knew I was coming. So did my brother Billy, but on Friday night Billy boy would be too busy cruising around in his van with the side pipes and spoiler and sun roof and Plexiglass tears at the rear. It was hot. I was already sweating. The old Victorian station had been remodeled inside but not yet air-conditioned. A low ceiling of hanging white panels hid those great high vaults and arches. But nice red carpets. Hertz and Avis. No more creaking floor boards, spits, butts, matches, and sailor puke.

I lockered my bag and walked up the short hill past the shop where an old Swede used to cut my hair. The place was now a toy store called The Happily Ever After: red letters on a bright yellow awning.

In the bar, I said, "Hey, hey, how's it going?" and pumped hands that belonged to a few familiar faces. I made my way to the end of the bar where Latch was. Almost seven feet tall, he was trim, still had his pionted beard and hair long in the back. Hooded eyes. Jok-

ingly, he grabbed my hand. I knew what was coming: "Nice to meet
you," he said. "Where in England are you from, Dulwich?"

"No, no, I'm just back from Osaka."

"Oh, Osaka. Let's see, that's . . . "

"Japan."

"Right. So you were in the Orient."

"All the time I was in Japan."

"Hey! I didn't know they knew you there."

"Oh, they know me. Don't worry. There were big turnouts."

"So you were big in Osaka."

"Very big, they loved me."

"What about Hokkaido?"

"Not to ask. Hokkaido is something else."

"We'll stick to Osaka."

"Good."

The routine had been good for lots of drunken hilarity. I laughed
soberly. Latch said to the kidface behind the bar, "Give my father
here a Bud."

Father. The word made me nervous. I wondered if it was a signal I
should say something, say I was sorry about his father. But Latch
quickly came back with some perfunctory questions about what I
was doing and how did I like my new job out West. I played it down,
said I was getting sick of moving around all the time. It was true.

"Beats Dulwich," he said, nodding toward the window.

"I wonder."

He laughed. "Now the night before you left last August. . . . "
I said we shouldn't talk about it.

He frowned in mock seriousness. "El stinko. You were *not* big in
Osaka, not that night."

"This is true."

He nudged a barmate. Ned went to school with us. Latch referred
to him as "Dulwich's Finest." I pumped his hand. The Ali fight was
just getting under way, in color, over the bar, and I could see he was
anxious. Latch said to him, "Ned, you remember Jake here."

"Sure, sure."

"He's just back from Osaka."

"Yeah?" He looked at me. "No shit?"

I nodded.

"Great place," said Latch, "beautiful women—he was very big."

"Where's this?"

"Osaka."

No lights went on in his dull heavy face.

Latch said, "It's off the coast of Nebraska."

"Great! You look great," said Ned. And back to Ali.

Latch let go with a bray of laughter.

Ned looked over his shoulder. "You fuckin' guys are crazy."

We watched the fight. I was in no hurry to get home. It would be easier to sneak in late. But I could feel myself getting on edge. The fight was not a good one. Beyond his prime, Ali had gotten fat, had lost his timing, was missing one too many shots. He spent most of his time on the dodge. It was hard to watch. Depressing. And the announcer kept calling the fight a fiasco, kept wondering what the Champ had left, if anything. I began to stare at myself in the bottles. During a commercial, Latch said something and I found myself saying, "I'm sorry about your father."

He laughed, made a joke of it. *"I'm* sorry *you're* sorry."

Ali barely won the fight. Guys in the bar were angry. Ned said, "I wish somebody'd kill that nigger."

Money changed hands.

"He's still champ," laughed one happy winner.

"But no longer big in Osaka," said Latch, evenly.

Things started to feel good. The bad joke was behind us. I wasn't thinking of anything. Two more foaming mugs were clunked down before us. The bar buzzed pleasantly.

"Let's see," said Latch, "what else have I got for you? Oh, yeah, Sloane's getting married."

"Impossible."

"True, but he is."

"That's the last of us then. Just you and me."

"Me, you mean. At least you gave it a shot."

"But it didn't last," I said.

"No matter. Confucius say, 'Think of whole.' "

We stared into our beers for a while. With mock seriousness, Latch said, "Your father and Billy will certainly be glad to see you." "Oh, yeah."

Two more mugs, all foam and frost. The bar was cool and comfortable. Things began to swim in a lovely weakness . . . the click and roll of balls . . . young peach-faces drifting above the emerald cloth . . . the lone coyote wail of some singer on the jukebox . . . the sailor and woman plotting adultery in one of the booths . . . a Gary Gilmore T-shirt saying LET'S DO IT. . . . My frosted mug seemed heavy and slippery and, by the time we were drinking up for the night, I had a funny feeling someone had nailed it to the bar, given me some kind of trick glass.

Outside, it was steamy. The moon followed us down the street and peeked over the rundown buildings by the Empire Theater, which had gone triple X-rated. A sign in red-on-white said: ADULT FILMS. Latch did a little zigzag walk and chanted, as we passed, "Let's all go to Osaka, let's all go to Osaka, let's all go to Osaka, and get ourselves a treat." Then, to me: "I-dentify that."

"Easy," I said. "Intermission. The old popcorn jingle."

A couple of black kids ran by, their sneakers whacking away on the sidewalk.

"No wonder you were big over there."

I told him he had a great chance. "After all, you are the original Big Fella."

We picked up my bag and drove out of town toward my father's house. We went through one of those strips packed with gas stations and burger joints, a long hellish neon corridor that petered out into darkness and branched into a road that ran between the Protestant and Catholic cemeteries. Latch offhandedly asked if I wanted to see where his father was. Thinking he meant the next day, I said yes, and he swerved under the big granite arch to St. Edward Cemetery.

The stones, washed white by the lights, sprang into view and stood there for a moment like the skyline of a crowded city that was suddenly around us and flowing past. I noticed expansion. Past the swan pond, the woods had been pushed back over a long hillside, exploding landmarks, mocking my old sense of limits. Latch at the wheel—he was smirking, almost as if he were doing it on purpose. In the last, most recent row of stones, next to a wall of trees, we pulled to a stop. We walked among the stones, each of us with a warm beer from Latch's supply in the car trunk. Teenagers again, here on some prank. A big moon lit the names quite clearly.

"Here they are," he said.

A gray stone, a double inscription marker: Emma Brownwiller 1910-1969; Carl Brownwiller 1908-1974. The last two digits were lighter gray. Lower down was a scroll with a sentiment phrase: "Lasting Regret." Cicadas were still hot in the trees. The can in my hand was almost hot, and I was dripping. In the distance, on the stretch between cemeteries, a biker was roaring, speed-shifting for the blind curve at the end. Standing there, looking at the stone, I recalled his father, a big man with a funny gash of a smile. Always active, he was usually in the yard, painting, mowing grass, repairing, even after he retired. "Good man," I said. "Great stories he told."

Latch snorted. "He was great to everybody but my mother." Moonlight caught his uptilted can. He swallowed. "Never took her out, spent any money on her. I think they hated each other. Hardly ever talked."

I said it was really hard to read other people's relationships, even with parents. But he didn't hear me. "After the second heart attack, I couldn't wait for him to die."

I must have flinched.

"Christ, don't be sentimental." There was a flash of irritation. "*Your* mother went like *that*"—he snapped his fingers—"but when you've got a hospital vigil, indifferent doctors, when you live day after day with your mother or father and see them get more and more like pale shadows, drugged, talking in circles, dragging up nasty old scenes, getting smelly, messing themselves—Christ, you get to hate them, you pray for their death."

It seemed best to say nothing.

"It's true," he said.

I sipped my beer. "Maybe so," I admitted, and realized I'd be sober for the rest of the night.

"Well, I'm finished with them now," he said. The tone was unconvincing.

It was quiet. A car came into the cemetery and shut off its lights in a distant alley. Parkers. It always struck me as a peculiar make-out place. Most marriages ended here; but, as I thought about high school, it occurred to me that some probably began here, in hot groaning back seats, under elegiac cedars and cypress. Latch walked toward a big feather-shaped cedar. "Remember DeVito?" he called.

I said yes. He owned a bar and served us before we were twenty-one, before beer turned teenage. "Come here," he said, laughed, and pointed at the stone. "For God's sake, don't get poetic on me."

DeVito. I asked how.

He laughed again, getting on my nerves. "He died—that's how. What the hell's the difference?"

We walked twenty feet this way and twenty that, Latch pointing out familiar names (one classmate), laughing all the time at my surprise, finally cackling. "Remember this guy?" He wasn't laughing anymore. The stone said "Clarence Geroux," one of our high school teachers. Latch's jaw moved from side to side, teeth grinding. He zipped down his fly. "I've always wanted to do this," he said, "and I can't think of a better grave." There was a long hiss as he squirted the stone. "Good old Mr. Geroux . . . Yes, Mr. Geroux . . . No, Mr. Geroux . . . Three classes with this prick . . . Taunted me so bad I had to cut . . . kept me out of college. . . . "

"You asshole, now you'll burn for sure. Sister Rose was right—you've come to no good end."

He grinned and stepped back. "Go on, give him some used Bud."

I told him I didn't have the urge. I was beginning to think of my father. Insects droned. The air was sweet. Latch drained his can of beer, crackled it. "Come on," I said, "Let's get out of here."

The gray face of the house rose above me. I watched Latch's red lights fade down the tree-lined street. My chin dripped. Cicadas kept saying "ski-oo, ski-oo," and I kept thinking "scare you, scare you." My brother's metallic red van with its hand-painted Arizona sunset and lone saguaro in black silhouette sat in the yard at a casual angle. No lights in the house. And when I got inside, no air. An old annoyance. My father easily had enough money for central air-conditioning but, as with so many other things, he was stubborn. Or was it oblivious? I began to realize just how much I wanted to drive him out of my mind, bury him: trips to Europe, jobs in distant places, yearly moving. Under the night light, on the kitchen counter was a new bottle of Cutty Sark, a half-killed Seagrams, a square-shouldered crystal decanter of vodka. Christ, why was I here? A stupid yearly ritual I couldn't break. Every time I came home, there was a new bottle of Cutty. Dad knew I liked it. Green glass and yellow label. Last time home, after only a few days, I noticed it was weak. "Watered" was a word that—making arrangements for myself—I would not pronounce.

I turned on a few lights and wanted to turn them off immediately: dustballs in the corners, dishes in the sink, cigarettes overflowing ashtrays in the den, coffee rings bitten into Mom's end tables, every surface with a film of dust. There was a scent of mildew all through the house. I went to the refrigerator for another beer and something to eat. There was a black banana, an overripe tomato oozing from its split, orange juice, milk, and a dozen beers. I closed the door and carried my bag upstairs.

In my old room, I got undressed, lay down, and waited for sleep. It didn't come, or only came in snatches. Heat was terrible. Sweat popped. I could feel it sliding down my ribs, dropping to the damp sheet. Several times my father did his nightwalk. The knob (loose) clunked, and the door creaked open. His clock-radio murmured away, stairs sounded as he made his way to the kitchen. The refrigerator hummed, then hummed more loudly when he opened the box. For a while nothing, almost as if he knew I were listening from the stair-head, straining. Then it came: the clank and pffft of the pulled tab. I went back to bed. Was he still punishing Mom? Like Latch pissing on Geroux's grave. Old age? Fear of oblivion? Too simple. He used to have friends, was king in a number of downtown bars, even after I turned twenty-one. He was especially big in the Hawk's Nest, which had a softball team. A good hitter and glove man. Well liked. Once a beautiful game-winning homer: a rising slow trajectory, the ball hanging for a moment in the tower lights and bugswirl before

diving out of sight behind the tall green fence. Toward dawn, after
Billy revved the engine and rumbled off down the street for work, I
fell asleep.

When I came down in the morning, he was sitting in the recliner,
aimed at the flickering TV. He was still in pyjamas, eyes small and
glassy and red and pouched, the world they saw, blurred, for his
glasses were gone. His face, so pale and so much older, scared me.
Arms behind his head, he just stared in the general direction of the
TV. Without hug or handshake, I was hurt. "Aren't you even going
to say hello to me?" I asked.

"Why should I?"

"Dad, what's the matter?"

"You know what's the matter." His face was ugly, twisted by
some inner corrosive. He shouted, "More than a month I didn't
hear from you."

I shouted back, "Christ, I was busy."

"Don't you shout at me, I'm your father." Then: "Sure, you're
always busy. Big Shot."

"Dad, I know kids who *never* call ——— "

"Sure, you know everything."

This was senseless. I wouldn't argue. Silence was better than the
yelling systematic way we pulled old scabs. I'd wait him out.
Sometimes that worked.

All morning long, he sat in front of the TV, chain-smoked. Coffee cup beside him, eating its rough bottom into Mom's end table.
Still in pyjamas. Sweat-reek blooming all around him. Anger filled
me and brimmed like water in a jar. I wanted to take him by the
neck. From room to room I walked, gorging myself on the dirt and
crust. I wanted to stick his nose in it and ask what about it. But that
wouldn't do. The curling odors, greasy sink—these were only symp-
toms.

I went outside. Beautiful day. Scent of pine resin from trees at the
side of the house. Nice and clean. Big, slow-moving clouds, cool as
ice-floes in that perfect blue sky. And Dad was mucking it all up, for
both of us. I watched a man who lived at the end of the street, a
retired navy man, sixtyish, in red shorts, come jogging up the road

and cut through the big field across the street. He had a tan and flashed me a healthy smile as he passed.

Later that afternoon, I was sitting in the living room, pretending to read the glossy magazine in my lap. He must have thought I was out. His recliner bumped the wall in the next room. Footsteps. There was a faint squeak of cork on glass, a hollow thoop. I could hear the vodka giggle into his cup.

"Dad," I said—his unshaven face turned toward me, the bottle still tipped—"For God's sake, Dad, what are you doing?"

Without a word, he turned and did that shuffling, uncertain walk back to his recliner, very deliberately placed the cup on the scarred wood, and flopped back, head-rest hitting the wall. He got a queer smile on his face, a look almost triumphant as he gazed, unseeing, at the game show where people were running around a stage, sticking their heads in buckets of water while the audience howled and gleefully shrieked. "Dad," I insisted, "talk to me. How long has this been going on?"

He remained smilingly mute.

"Dad, why are you doing this?"

Finally, he said, "I have my reasons." His words were thick.

"What reasons? There are no good reasons for this."

"For what? You didn't come in drunk last night? Hooked up with Latch, didn't you?"

"That's different and you know it."

"Sure, everything's different for you."

"Dad."

Nothing.

"Dad, I love you." I knelt and touched his hand, squeezed it.

Nothing. Then: "Sure you do. You're a fast one with words. Charm the fuzz off a peach. People that think you're so nice—they ought to know you. You're just like your mother, your sweet mother. You always took her part, not mine. Never mine!"

I half-listened. It was an old routine about how Mom's family was much bigger than his, more clannish, and how they never really accepted him or recognized his accomplishments, how her brother once—because Dad didn't have the credit—charged him higher than bank interest on a loan, how Dad had a big job in the western part of

the state and her family forced them in various ways to come back,
how Mom never liked any of his friends and resented his winning way
with strangers.

"Dad, I know, but this is ancient history."

"Oh, you know it all, that's for sure." He sneered, his face
quivering, red. "Just remember *I* paid for what you know."

"I'm grateful," I said.

"You have never been grateful."

"I *have.*"

"In a pig's ass . . . think your education came from your
mother? Tight as wallpaper, like the rest of her family. *I, me,* I
wanted it."

"I know, Dad."

"You don't know."

I told him I had heard all this before and it was, right now, beside
the point. Why was he drinking himself to death—that was the only
point I was interested in.

He said nothing, sat there in his faded blue pyjamas. I could smell
his body, an odor of decay snaking about me. "Are you going to
throw in the towel?" I asked. "Hell, there are men older than you
who run every year in the Boston Marathon, play tennis,
everything."

Nothing.

"Remember what you used to say to me about quitters?"

Finally he said, very deliberately, "You don't know anything."

His judgment of me seemed so final I shuddered.

I walked around the yard and into a piney woods behind our
house. How long had this been going on? I replayed visits of the past
for telltale signs, but the footage, such as it was, was spotty. And I
realized that memory, if you have not observed closely, cannot
speak her secrets. I was stuck with the facts. What to do? Alcoholics
Anonymous, a psychiatrist, a drying-out resort—but these options
work only for people who want them to work. And no matter what
he said, I knew my father, knew also that I was too much a part of
the problem to be of much help. The parish priest briefly came to

mind: he was a tall, dark, arrogant man, a Sunday morning bari-
tone, a scold. Father Zindt. Thrashing me in grammar school. Dad
thrashing me again at home, telling me I had to respect the priests
and nuns. And Dad no longer going to church. Hypocrite. And
about drinking too. How he scorned my mother's brother who died
a drunk in the VA hospital. And landing on me for my drinking with
Latch. Now look at *him.* He stood in the window, perhaps watching
me with pleasure as I went casting about the yard and woods. *You
don't know anything.* His pale face, half-hidden in the reflections of
moving pine boughs, stared into a private bitter trance. There was a
rusty rake leaning against the house, and I wanted to take it in my
hands, break the window, reach in, and drag him through the fangs
of glass.

That evening, Billy appeared: "Hey, man." As if he saw me
every day. Unable to think of anything else to say, I asked him about
Dad's drinking. He shrugged. Billy had my mother's big, sad,
moist, brown eyes, only his were unfocused and glassy most of the
time from pot, and the sadness was offset by a hard, smirking
mouth. He came in her change of life, was separated from me by a
dozen years. "He don't drink much," he said.
I said, "I don't think you've been looking closely."
He shrugged again.
"You buy the booze?"
"Right, to keep the peace."
I wondered if he knew what peace was.
"Hey, don't worry about what I know."
I asked why Dad had it in for me.
"I don't know," he said. "He never discusses it."
"Really?"
"Hey, I'm telling ya." He was fidgeting. I was making him ner-
vous. I asked him why he didn't try to stop Dad's drinking. "You
should quit buying the stuff," I said.
"Look, man"—his mouth crimped at the corners—"he knows
what he's doing."
"Does he?"

"He's an adult, isn't he?"

"Good, maybe we should get him some"—I winked lewdly—"adult magazines for his old age, straighten him out."

A tense quiet. "You're fucked up," he said. "You always have to joke."

"I'm not joking, just a little mad."

"I'm not either. Look, man, he's into juice. That's his thing. I'm not going to stop him."

"I know, man, and you're into dope," I told him, mocking his idiom.

He made a contemptuous mouth.

"Latch told me you got arrested."

"Oh, Latch is a good one to talk. How many times has he been busted?"

"So what happened?"

"A little grass, no big thing."

I recalled my own early brushes with the cops and how my name in the paper shamed Dad in front of his workmates. "What did Dad say?"

"I don't think he knew. Can't read without his glasses."

And what the hell was this about the glasses I asked.

"I don't know. He keeps saying he'll get new ones. If you remind him, he gets mad."

"Why won't he get new ones?"

"How the hell do I know?"

We were out in the yard. I looked off at the low sun, at the treeline. Give him a space to calm down. Then I asked him about the pyjamas and if he always stayed in. Billy said no. Last winter they went to a few basketball glames. Sometimes they went out to a restaurant. And I wondered if he behaved this way only when I came home. A way of getting at me. Or poor dead Mom. Or something. *You don't know anything.* I became aware of Billy saying " . . . the fuck is this? I don't know what we talked about. Just things, sports. I don't know. That's it, man. No more. You're making a big thing outta nothin'."

It was the straw I was waiting for. "I hope you're right," I said.

For the remainder of my week visit, I heard that terrible squeak and thoop at odd times. I escaped several times with Latch, but mostly I watched the levels of those bottles on the counter fall until one was replaced and the decanter magically refilled itself at night. The Cutty remained uncracked. But my father's eyes were cracked, seemed to grow smaller in his pale face as he gazed at the TV with a blank expression, layers of gray smoke writhing about his head and neck, coiling.

I cooked some meals and washed dishes. Did some cleaning on the sly. He said nothing. I suggested we go out to a nice restaurant. He spoke, only to refuse, sitting there in his faded blue pyjamas. And that's where I left him.

The stainless steel side of the coach was splattered with mud, dulled with grit. After a night flight from Chicago, I caught the train in New York, sat and stared at an image of my father in his trance. It rained and rained, all the way home. I walked through the station to a taxi out front. "Can you take me out to Chester?"

"Yup, get in."

I spotted The Happily Ever After as we pulled out.

"What's so funny?" asked the driver.

I didn't answer. There were silver points of fear in his eyes. And he spoke no more.

My father's last bitter trump—it came from his lawyer before the funeral—was that he be buried with *his* family in Chester. There was a short hand-scrawled note to me: "You were your Mama's boy. Keep the plot beside her for yourself, forever." Why? Why not simply cut me out if he hated me? Billy and I, it turned out, would share the estate. Dad's spiteful gesture didn't make sense, or was that the sense that it made? Had he just wanted me to come home? Was that it?

You don't know anything.

It hummed in the mind. Like the bees that hung above the funeral flowers in the yellowing watery air once the rain had stopped. It was infernally hot. Cicadas wailing. A gothic cemetery. The grave was in line with those of my grandmother and grandfather; it was next to a fence of tall, black iron spears. The priest stood alone at the head of the varnished casket, a droning, red-wattled vulture. I walked a

Kennedy half-dollar between my knuckles. There were reddish
stones, some with scabs of gray-green lichen, a swamp just below
with tall cat o' nine tails, green, several bent by redwing blackbirds.
Nimbly, the half-dollar went in and out of my knuckles. A reprov-
ing look from my aunt. I did the classic pass and made it vanish,
showed empty hands. Still, she frowned. So I reached over and
made it appear behind my uncle's ear. "Amen," said Father
Somebody. The device was tripped, and on canvas straps the box
settled heavily downward with its awful cargo. But I didn't look. He
was still in the recliner with a blank face. He could see me in this
yellow heat, look from the window with that triumphant idiotic
grin. I wouldn't be made a fool of. Which hand was the coin in?
Neither. See? From a tree in the swamp, starlings hit the air like bits
of exploded hearse. Latch stood on the other side, above the heads,
mopping his face with a white handkerchief. My uncle, shiny
blisters of sweat on his forehead, turned for the funeral car, his summer gray all dark down the back. A man in a boxy suit with great
wide lapels held open the car door. And shut it. A dim vinyl gloom.
He started the engine, and cold air rushed from the vents. Billy
sneezed. In the next alley an old pickup with three young diggers
waited impatiently. We rolled out and onto a country road, empty
except for an old man in a straw hat and white shirt. He was starting
up a long hill in the whitening light.

It was important to keep moving, focus.
Billy and I carried an old door from the damp cellar up to the
knoll under the pines where there was a carpet of bronze needles.
Any chance of a breeze would be there. The door made a table between two scarred sawhorses. Old days making things in the cellar
with Dad. Jigsawed animals. Birdhouses. I went into the kitchen for
the fifths of whiskey. Billy put a sheet over the door. We had done
the same for Mom and her brother. Ironically, most of Mom's clan
was present. Latch helped with a few cases of beer, tubbed and iced
them under the door. He paused. How was I doing? I laughed. In
Osaka? His face shifted, eyes widened. Relatives and neighbors
were slamming car doors and trudging up the grade with platters of
salad, cheese, cold cuts. Wasps kept landing on food, pulsing their

lethal abdomens. People loading and balancing the bendy paper plates. Hot pine pinched the nostrils. Groups formed. Drinks went down. Voices rose. Everyone assured each other it was hot. Otherwise a lovely day. People approached me cautiously and addressed comments. I didn't look at their faces, I looked at their hands. Miss Peg had long narrow hands, white as soap carvings, with wrinkled backs and bulgy veins the color of ink on a certificate of death. The hands parted with strain, snapped together as if by a magnet. Predictably she said that Dad looked lovely laid out. I said he had embalmed himself. The hands fretted. Yes, did it himself with 100 proof Smirnoff. They jerked. The mortician only had to comb his hair. Mr. Burns, our neighbor, had one hand pocketed, the other, liver-spotted, curled about a plastic glass. That back surgery, he said. Seven years ago your father was a different man. My cousin's little girl asked for Pepsi. I went to the cellar. Nellie, Mom's best friend, had delicate hands, long slim fingers, balletic gestures. Why? she repeated, paused. Friction is like love for some people. Without her he was lost. Aunt Mary said he had lost his faith, but everyone prayed and in the end Father Zindt was there. Uncle Bill said no: Dad *never* had much use for the Church. Their hands, red, flapped at each other like fighting cocks. Uncle Ed said I ought to show respect. Magic has its place. His hands were big and square and tanned; the fingers were thick, nails broken and rimmed with slim moons of dirt. One jumped on my shoulder. The other hoisted a glass nearly full of straight Four Roses, two dime-sized cubes disappearing. I said Dad taught me those tricks; it was a form of prayer. Honest. You need a drink, he said. *You don't know anything.* It tickled, started my dry cackle. You ought to have a drink, he said. Somebody else said Billy and I should get out of that house; it was unhealthy. My cousin Dean said nothing. He rolled a piece of bologna into a tube and popped it into his mouth; he ate with his mouth open so you could admire the way it mixed with the chewed cracker and tumbled about like dirty clothes in a port-holed washer. He laughed and washed it down with a beer. Dad watched from the window with a triumphant grin half-hidden in reflections. What did I know? I knew hands. They were thick and thin knuckled, fat and slim fingered, white and tanned, hairy and smooth, ringed and ringless; they dangled at sides, flew to each other, held elbows, twitched, dug in noses, thoughtlessly lifted food, came indifferently to itches, lay inertly on chair arms—they led a reckless, imcomprehensible life of their own.

Next day I found myself carting the garbage cans out to the street. An awful stench came out of them; they weren't full, but I couldn't face a heaving whiteness of maggots so I drove Dad's old Ford to the back of a plaza TV store for boxes. The car was filthy and dead-smelling with dust and had an ashtray of cascading butts, a smeary windshield. Returning, I pulled the car under the pines, opened both doors, and cleaned it completely, giving the interior a wash with Lysol, mostly for scent. I'd wax a small section of it everyday so that at least one part of my day would be X-ed in, and looming ahead sometime would be the image of a '55 Ford restored to a former state of shining integrity. Maybe. But it was my car now.

Then I attacked the house, opening all the windows. An empty cardboard box in each room. First I collected the crucifixes with palm fronds, yellow-brown, that were coiled around them. Into the box. Even the Extreme Unction kit—a hollow cross—with salt and oil and a tiny towel and candles inside. Then the statues and holy pictures of the Blessed Mother, The Sacred Heart, St. Theresa, St. Jude, The Infant of Prague (this one gotten up with a gold crown and a red satin cape with fake ermine trim), and St. Joseph. Into the box. I carried the box down to the street and dropped it next to the barrels. The plaster statues clinked and off went the head of St. Joe.

Working slowly, deliberately, taking short jaunts into town for real and imaginary necessities, I reshaped the house while my brother worked. I had decided to stay and would make the house my own. At night, Billy grunted approval but said little.

Finally, I arrived at Dad's room, that private sanctum, open to scrutiny at last. I opened drawers in the oak dresser, nervously, as if he might suddenly appear in the doorway, bellow, and get me by the neck with his big hands for daring to spy on his life. Into the box went stained underwear, sleeveless T-shirts, faded pyjamas, a bath-robe, handkerchiefs, socks, a scarf, and shirts. In the top drawer I found a Social Security card, a driver's license, a union membership card, dues receipts, two old wallets, and the one he used to the end (no snapshots, nothing personal). In a small jewelry box made of cardboard covered with silver foil, resting on cotton, were their wedding bands, pale gold, peaceful, side by side. Quick, I had to put them aside. There were other things in the drawer: clasps, stickpins, cuff links—most were greenish with oxidation. Into the box. Two large manila envelopes stuffed with family pictures—those I would look at later, study. It was hot. A fly buzzed against the upper part of the window, was caught in the curtains. I was tempted to quit. But where were those girlie books, that pack of porno cards that would help fill in the picture? Here was a letter postmarked Chester, 1930, addressed to Dad at a rooming house in Providence. I think he worked for a man who moved houses. The letter was in Polish, from my grandmother. Probably nothing. I went on looking. Where were they, those telltale letters from another woman? Or letters from Mom to Dad when he was in the service? Or letters from Mom's lover? Evidence—where was it?

I started on the closet, the floor. Dead shoes, a black umbrella filled with dust, fallen wire hangers, tongueless rubbers, cracked boots, a fallen necktie, one of Mom's forgotten purses (an Indian head nickel inside), a warped tennis racket (I recalled a browning snapshot of Dad toweling off at the net, smiling), some metal shoe trees. Into the box. And a half-empty bottle of Seagrams. Dad's only unfinished project. Christ, why couldn't he have emptied it? He could have left a note in bold black strokes: "Ave atque vale." That would have been style. Into the box.

I stood up. The box was filling with bits of his life. Now the coats and suits that hung like thin slabs of dark meat from the wire hangers. Finally, when I had pulled everything from the closet—like entrails—there was a strange cane hanging on the pipe by its crook. It was black and had a number of inlaid pearl designs: flowers. Looked oriental. I had never seen it before, and there it was, suddenly, a kind of hanging menace. In my hands, it had an odd balance. I noticed a joint-seam in the brass collar at the neck. Sure, it was one of those canes with a sword inside. Holding it horizontally, I grabbed the scabbard and twisted the handle. There was a violent report, smoke, a piece of black flak shooting past my head and bouncing back. My ears rang. The room echoed. Then I saw myself holding the cane, a hole of daylight at my heart, a radiating web of silver lines in the window glass, my hand trembling at the look of my father's idiotic smile. *You don't know anything.*

When I showed Billy the cane, he, too, said he had never seen it. "But it's really far-out, hunh? A .22, single shot."

"What would Dad be doing with that?"

Billy said, "I give up." He inspected it closely, eyes wide with excitement. I explained how the rubber tip ricocheted off the wall. "You must of shit."

"You wouldn't?"

"Sure." He swung and aimed it at the woods. "Hey, maybe he got it in the service."

I said that was possible, but why?

"Why does there always have to be a *why*? Just to have it, is all. Waste a burglar maybe."

"Was Dad ever in Japan?"

He hoisted his eyebrows. "Beats me."

Billy insisted on firing it again. He put a tin can on the wall where the woods began. There was an unconvincing bang, and a tick, tick, tick, as the bullet ran through sundown leaves.

Life fell into a pattern of fast-food meals, car-work, bar-haunting, and sleep. Lots of sleep, especially after a beery night with Latch and the boys. After a while, the Ford shone, but there were a number of spots too badly oxidized to be restored. I bought points, plugs, and condenser and with Billy's timing light got the engine to hum. Then what? A vacuum. Finally, I looked in those two manila envelopes, winced, but kept looking. In browning photos, Mom and Dad smiled at me from where they were once very happy. That was it. What happened to them happened after I went away to college, slowly, not dramatically. Then Mom died and whatever it was, worsened. Dad retired, and the house became empty, full of time, space, and memory. It was too much for him. For me. I took to walking around from room to room, notion to notion, with that loaded cane to protect me—protect me from the eerie reaches of the house about me, from my father's genes within me, coiled in their darkness, ready to strike. I sat in the recliner. At night, everything wore a look of fatigue, and the room seemed to breathe, the walls expand and contract like lungs. Furniture was alien, a clutter of oddments ingested by a whale. One night, the doorbell rang in another world. I grabbed the cane and looked out the window: it was Latch.

We sat in Irene's, a downtown bar. Some guys in green-and-white softball uniforms ganged in from a victory. Lots of laughing and drinking. Big gold pitchers of beer beaded with sweat. I thought of Dad's homer, that beautiful white trajectory, the ball hanging at its peak. Latch signaled the bartender for two more. "Church education," he snarled. "Thou shalt love death with thy whole heart."

"My father didn't buy that spiel."

"Don't be so sure. What about your mother?"

"She was different."

"And what about *you*?"

"Don't taunt me."

"Anyway, it's too early to tell," he taunted. "Like with drugs, poisons. Think of women on the Pill. Everyday I expect to see my sister with another eye in the middle of her forehead."

We laughed. The bar was quieting down for a championship bout: it was Ali again.

"Only one thing you can be sure of," said Latch. "One thing."

"What's that?"

"Once upon a time, we were all very big in Osaka." He knocked back the beer and laughed in his black way. "Oh, yeah, once upon a time."

Above the bar, Ali, in red trunks, looked great. The belt of fat was gone from his middle. His timing was back, and he was throwing shots—jabs, hooks, combos—from everywhere. He floated, circled, reversed direction, dropped his hands, faked beautifully, and clowned just enough to remind you who he was. After Ali had taken a few heavy punches, someone said, "That's it, he's finished. Hasbeen City here he comes." But even in the later rounds, he was on his toes, full of grace, and fighting.

Don't Call Us, We'll Call You

Leon slouched in the canvas patio chair and watched the sweat seethe and pop on his tan upper arm, gather into tiny runnels, slide, snag, and slide again through the bleached hairs; then it pooled at the joint and trickled down his tennis elbow and dripped, as if from a broken pipe. He looked up, finally, at the Spanish moss that until a week ago he had only seen in movies. Strange, eerie, the long gray strands hung absolutely still from pine and cypress over the black river. The gray made Leon think of his own hair, which had recently streaked. Friends he had left up North made the usual comments—that he looked more mature, handsome, dignified, and all that. But he knew better; none of the descriptions fit. It was mere chitchat, the kind he was listening to now. Sherry was saying, vaguely, they would have to get together for a cookout.

"Yes, we should," said Georgette.

"Do you and Leon like fish?" asked Sherry.

Georgette said they did.

"Good, we do too."

"Anything but red snapper," said Georgette.

"I know a great seafood place ———"

"Which is in New York," said Duke.

"Yes," said Sherry with a laugh. "That's right."

"This is Georgia," said Duke. "Remember?"

"Yes," said Sherry, playing along and sucking a little-girl finger. They laughed nervously.

Georgette, as usual, came back to her thought: red snapper.

Plodding up the brick stairs to the kitchen, glasses in hand, Leon heard her say the word *bouillabaisse,* tell how in Marseille one summer she informed the waiter she wouldn't have snapper in her fish chowder. Christ, they were coming on all wrong with these new people; already there had been too much hey-look-at-us. Leon mopped his face with a sheet of green paper towel. With the air-conditioner broken and clothing pasted to his skin, binding, he felt disgustingly fat. And sick of himself, his voice, his anecdotes. Four times in five years the company had moved him, forced him into these repetitions. The refrigerator door made a sucking thump. Leon broke the back of the ice tray, and oval cubes, smelling of swamp water, rained into the blue plastic bucket. A window over the sink framed and held the patio and the director's chairs of white wood and yellow canvas, the tall unpainted plank fence, and the two brickwork gateposts. Beyond the open gate was a short expanse of brownish grass, then the black river sliding along in its slot, overhung by the motionless gray moss. The sky was still lit but quickly losing its tints of rose and peach, and against the dark trees, fireflies, here and there, began to test their lights. The air was feverish with swamp noise. A police launch burbled slowly upstream; it listed to one side as a big fat man chewed on a stubby cigar and peered into the murky waters. A black woman was supposed to have leaped from the cantilever bridge in the center of town. All day, from shore and boat, they had been throwing a grappling hook. Ploosh. Then heave and haul. Leon could see it bumping along the bottom, snagging, then lunging with four bare prongs for a thigh, groin, breast, face.

He twisted his mouth into a smile. "Here," he said to Duke, handing him a bourbon. "This'll set you free."

And slumped onto his chair.

"Thanks," said Duke, soberly, and crossed his legs. He was tall, gaunt, and had a round head of short sandy hair, a sensitive profile. Leon was taken with the face: active, witty-looking, composed. Tricky light hid the color of the pupils, which were caught in a web of red threads. Duke was curious. Actually, they were both curious, different: Duke in his coarse white caftan, Sherry with her cigarillo. Sherry, too, was slim and tan; she looked younger than she probably was, with shaggy frosted hair that hugged her skull like a bathing cap. "Hot enough for you?" she asked Leon.

Leon sighed, "Whew!"

Georgette said, "Christ, I wish it would snow," in her brassy way.

Leon asked if it got any hotter.

"July and August," said Duke, inspecting his fingernails.

"August, hunh?" repeated Georgette.

"It's always a hundred," said Sherry.

"Incredible humidity with the river," added Duke. He still inspected his nails. There were faint twists of amusement at the corners of his narrow mouth.

Leon said, "Hell, quit torturing us!"

They laughed. Sherry drew on her cigarillo until the tip was scarlet, bubbled her cheeks, and blew a big pewter smoke ring, which hung perfectly for a long moment. When it was gone, she said, "Oh, you'll get used to it."

Duke smiled mysteriously.

"How long have you been here?" asked Georgette.

Duke checked his watch. "About thirty-five minutes."

Georgette said, "Naw, *you* know what I *mean*," and did her raspy laugh.

Leon looked at the river. What was their game? Their talk seemed subtly barbed, tricky. An outboard droned, grew into view, and labored past; it was a slow-moving white ghost with a red running light that Leon watched until it was snuffed by the bend. The pilot had been invisible. He thought of the black woman and worked into his glass of bourbon. When a moment of talkless quiet widened, he felt, against some other instinct, a need to fill it. "I wonder," he found himself saying, "if heat really makes Southerners slower."

"Than Northerners?"

"No . . . Martians!"

Everyone laughed.

"I wonder," mused Sherry, biting the inside of her cheek.

Duke said, "You tend not to exert yourself in the heat."

"You see them fanning and rocking all the time," said Georgette.

"On porches," added Sherry.

"Yes," said Duke. He paused. "You see them on country porches."

"Christ," said Georgette, "we ought to live in the car until the goddamn air-conditioner is fixed."

"You wonder what people did *before* air-conditioners," said Sherry, amused at the triteness.

"Yes, I *know*," said Georgette, catching on.

Leon had an urge to tell about two blacks who, that afternoon, came to repair the air-conditioner but ended, as in a TV skit, by making things worse, by breaking the fan altogether. They were young. One had his hair in that corn-row style; there were little pigtails knitted tightly all over the skull, lots of seams, like a volley ball. The other wore a green wool ski cap; he had sweat running off his chin, like a faucet. The temperature was close to a hundred, and here was this guy in a ski cap. Funny details, turns, ironies. But these people might not take it well. Leon's clowning was sometimes painful. He had not heard from his old friend, Joe, since the wedding where, at the hotel bar, he had needled him about the "coon" couple who had been invited. God, the memory made him wince. Why did he say such things? He had to be more careful. Now he would be calling at stores like Dixie, Dixon's, Higson's, Tyson's, Buck's— strange names, perhaps even stranger people. He didn't know. Southerners, he had been told, were formal and polite. They would require a different approach. But even with northerners one should never assume. No, he had better not tell about the blacks. Instead, he would punctuate what Sherry just said about the South being another country; he stood up and, leaning backward, he clamped his thick fingers over imaginary lapels and imitated the great nasal slurring of W. C. Fields: "Indeed, indeed."

Everyone laughed.

Leon leaned toward Sherry: "You're empty."

"So I am."

"Let me fill you up."

"Thanks."

The kitchen was very still. Here he was more himself—sad, gloomy. He flicked on the orange bug-light atop the brickwork post. Again the window held the same three figures, and his empty chair. Let the chair remain empty. Hide from the Fields gag. Why did he always have to play the clown? A queer, sharp, painful cry sounded, suddenly, twice quickly, from the dim tree-rim across the narrow river and, after a few moments, it came again from farther down river, somewhat muted. His hand, on the Jim Beam bottle, hesitated. What the hell was it? But no one noticed. His chair was empty. And the talk went on. Duke and Sherry were polite; they had poise; they knew what was *supposed* to be funny and did their duty, laughed moderately. Through the window he watched Duke who, leaning on one elbow, crossed his legs and gestured with his cigarillo as he spoke. Leon's eyes smarted with sweat. It stung him the more to notice that the others seemed cool in spite of the heat. With only a hint of moisture on his skin, Duke tilted his round head in a kind of squinty consideration as he listened to Georgette, as a shrink might. But now she was popping the questions, filling her file.

"Undergraduate school?"

"Yes."

"NYU."

"Oooh."

Sherry said, "Ask me too." They seemed like children playing a game.

"Okay. Where did *you* go to undergraduate school?"

"NYU."

"Hey!"

"Hey!"

Leon wished he could simply watch through the window, listen. Moths made flapping, unpredictable orbits around the orange lamp. The river followed its deep alarming groove, unseen. Leon wished he could be more laconic, like Duke, his brother-in-law, and a few other magnetic types he knew. He was soaked; he mopped his face with another leaf of green paper towel. Never had he so little desire to be with people. To return to the patio suddenly seemed like betraying some bit of residual value in himself.

Sherry lifted her face. "Thanks."

"Did you check on the kids?" asked Georgette.

He said, "It's been pretty quiet up there." He simply had to keep his talk to a minimum, hold back, play it like Duke.

"So," said Georgette. "NYU."

"Yup." Sherry sipped her fresh drink, the cubes tinkling. "Hit me," she said, leaning toward Duke who shook loose another cigarillo, which she deftly plucked from the pack. They laughed. Some private joke. Leon squirmed in his chair. Looking at her tanned, sturdy body, the curves, planes, and the high color of her face, he could not believe that he was really here, near the Georgia coast, in this oven heat, listening to these exchanges, facing these strangers. Only a week ago he was in Boston. Like being a pebble on the leather of a slingshot; you never knew who would fling you, or where, or when. But the uncertainty of leaving the company was too much to think about.

"NYU, is that where you two met?"

"Come on," said Leon. "You sound like the Dating Game."

Georgette turned, ice clunking in her glass, and said very casually, "Maybe you'd rather tell some of your macho stories. Or how you were a high school bad-ass."

Sherry barked into her hand.

Leon ground his molars, forced a grin.

Duke chuckled. "Were you one of *them*?"

Leon nodded.

"Oh boy, just ask him," said Georgette. She rolled her eyes. "Anyway, where was I?"

"How did we meet?" offered Sherry.

"That's right. How did you meet? *If,* of course, you don't mind." She cut her eyes to Leon.

They didn't mind. It was easy. They were both teaching assistants in the Speech and Drama department.

"At NYU?"

"At NYU."

"Ahhh," sighed Georgette, as if she were at last getting somewhere.

"How about you?" asked Duke. "How did you two meet?"

Leon cringed; he never knew how far her dark humor would take her.

"Well," began Georgette, "we were in the same department

too—the clothing department at Filene's!'' She threw her head back and gave that raw beefsteak laugh of hers.

Leon tried to keep his face limber, amused.

"Not really though—I just said that for a laugh." She leaned forward for her drink on the glass-topped table. "Actually, I was a buyer. Leon came in every other week. One of those things."

"To Filene's?"

"I bought, he sold." Georgette paused. "In fact, he sold me more and more—more than I was supposed to buy."

"Until you bought *him,*" Sherry put in, giggling into her glass.

"Riiight!"

"What did you study in college?" asked Duke.

"Marketing."

"What about you, Leon?"

"Well," coughed Leon, "you won't believe this but . . . would you believe philosophy?"

"No kidding."

"Really."

"*Really?*"

"Really."

"How about that."

"Interesting," said Sherry. She slid her eyes, furtively toward Duke.

Leon bit his lip. A swap of indulgent looks? He couldn't tell.

"Philosophy," mused Duke. "I *think,* therefore I *am*—an underwear salesman!"

"Hey!"

"Hey!"

"No," protested Leon. "I *think,* therefore I *drink.*"

And exit.

The cubes thunked into glasses. The bottle tipped, liquor splashed. Moths bumped against the glass panes of the lamp, trying to touch the light. Leon wondered where he stood with these people. There had been humor but with it, he felt, a certain mockery, keen and thin as a needle. Maybe not. But they were hard to read. From far down river came that cry again, sharp, two quick notes that pierced the fabric of darkness. Beyond the fence were the random pricks of fireflies. From philosophy to Fruit of the Loom. This had always been good for laughs, but now it was profoundly unfunny, painful. There was something about Duke and Sherry that made it so.

Leon returned to the patio, handed glasses around. Crickets seemed to throb more loudly. Sherry was telling about the first place they lived when they came to town, about a guy on their street. " . . . gun . . . everyone . . . boy next door . . . crying . . . comes back. . . . " Leon tilted his chair against the fence, watched the three bunched cubes in his glass shift, lean, and finally float, drift. He wanted nothing so much as to stare at his drink, thoughtlessly, forget the dark panels of shirt pasted to his skin, forget the image he had of himself as a baked potato set on toothpick legs. People at the apartment pool were lean, lively, intense in conversation. Leon felt tired. " . . . about six years old . . . crossed the yard with his father's deer rifle . . . aims at the little boy he had just argued with . . . before anyone can react . . . the father now, slow as you please, comes up and retrieves the gun from Duke and tells him—get this—tells him he ought to mind his own business."

The story at last caught Leon's attention. "What did *you* say?" He was looking at Duke.

Duke arched his eyebrow. "Like the song says, 'You can't talk to a man with a shotgun in his hand.' " He closed his eyes and shrugged.

"Didn't the father," Georgette asked, "say anything to the kid?"

"Just something like, 'What I done tole you,' and that was it."

"No apologies, explanations, nothing?"

"Nothing."

Leon hooted, "Welcome to Chor-ja. Y'all come back, hear?" But as soon as he heard his words, he knew he had betrayed himself, again, through levity.

Duke said, "Let's be fair, though. Worse happens in New York all the time. I lived there for six years, and we saw some pretty terrible things."

Sherry nodded. "That's right."

"One night, coming back from a party, we came out of the subway, and there was a man lying on the sidewalk. This was———"
Duke pressed his fingertips together, his eyes squinted, far-focused.
"This was in January. Freezing night. I knew he was alive because I could see vapor coming from his mouth. At first I thought, heart attack. Then he groaned and propped himself on his elbow. His coat fell open, and I saw blood on his shirt. Slash marks. Then you noticed a little blood pool forming." Leon looked at the gaunt face, hollow eyes, red veins. All irony seemed gone. Georgette and Sherry, like twins, sat with mouths slightly pursed, lips parted, ready to move, as Duke imitated the man lifting his hand. "He looked at me with the kind of look you would like to forget and kind of lifted his arm. I wanted to help him but, I'm ashamed to say, I didn't. I was afraid. His other hand was in his pocket, fumbling."
Duke paused; his eyes casted, as if he had been saying lines and needed a prompt. "Well, I backed away. Maybe, in his dazed condition, he thought I was a hood come back to finish the job. Maybe the guy himself was a hood and had a knife or a gun in that pocket. I didn't know. I was afraid to take a chance. It was an incredibly helpless feeling. And a few passersby look at you like maybe *you* did this guy in. So there you are: you *know* you should do something, you *want* to do something, but your practical sense says no." Leon watched him draw his hands to his chest, turn them up, palms empty, like someone asking for something. "We backed away, watching his mouth open, the whites of his eyes take over."

"A block or so away," said Sherry, "we found a cop and went back with him."

Duke said simply, "The guy was dead."

"It was horrible," said Sherry. Her face was stricken.

Something splashed in the river. Leon stared at the moths circling the glass of the lamp, trying to get at the light. Duke said, "I'm not sure what my point is . . . or was. Just, I guess, that there are as many lunatics in New York as Georgia. Maybe more. Maybe that wasn't my point either. I don't know.

But the story, with the image of the man, toes up, on an empty winter sidewalk of New York, dying, affected Leon powerfully.

And as Duke spoke, something revealing entered his face, as if it were his own father he had been talking about. Duke was redeemed. Leon now felt differently about Duke and Sherry. He wanted to reinforce, reveal that he too knew that unspoken thing. "I think I know," said Leon. "You can find it anywhere. The violence, I mean." He bit his lip; he meant more than he could easily say. He began again. "I had a neighbor. What a neighbor! He was a gun-freak too. Different though."

"Very different," put in Georgette.

"It was a family of poor whites. They lived across an empty lot from us. An unpainted shack, you know? They flung trash into the back yard and burned it every few weeks. But the real thing had to do with the dogs. They had four beagles, on chains. Anything would set them howling. After a while, Homer—that was his name—Homer would come out the back door and bellow something, and they would get quiet again. Sometimes he'd just kick one until all you could hear was squealing and yelping. Good ole Homer. He was only a few years younger than me. His wife, though, was *sixteen* and she had *two* kids."

"Sixteen going on forty," said Georgette, "is how she looked. They were strange people. Unpredictable. Really, don't laugh. One day you'd wake up and from nowhere there would be a horse tied to the apple tree in the lot. Or maybe you'd look out the window and see a deer strung up on this gismo he used to pull the motor out of his car with. Or you'd discover another junk car. No end to it."

Leon sat forward, put down his drink, and dangled his hands over his knees. He let the quiet construct a serious mood; it might atone for the clownish things said before; it would tell Duke something. "Well, this one snowy Sunday afternoon I was upstairs at my desk. I was supposed to be writing a sales report, but I couldn't get into it. Instead I was reading some Tolstoy. Georgette and the girls were downstairs doing something quiet. I must have been enjoying the book because the shot bolted me out of my chair. I hustle to the window. Nothing is moving. Everything is covered with snow and any movement you could see right off, you know?"

Duke and Sherry nodded in unison.

"I began to wonder if it wasn't just a car backfiring. But the

sound seemed to come from the backyard. In any case, I went back
to Tolstoy. Five minutes later, another shot. This time I get there in
time to see the collie in mid-leap, rearing up, bending around like it
was trying to bite at its back legs. I also saw the gun barrel zip into
Homer's back door. The dog disappeared behind this old garage-
barn behind our house. It came out running, but half way across our
yard its back legs buckled. By the time I got to the other window, it
was up again and in a panic, it ran straight into the chain link fence
on our north side. Well, for a while, I didn't know what to do.''
Leon looked at Duke, then noticed his hands as they flapped like
shot doves, a picture of alarm. ''I just stood there and watched the
dog try to find its feet again. Made you think of a broken toy.''
Leon bit his lip. ''It just lay there thrashing in the snow. Took about
ten minutes to die. When I got outside, I still couldn't do anything.
The dog was snapping and had its teeth bared. You couldn't get near
him. Besides, a lot of its rear end had been shotgunned away. I tried
to keep a few kids on the street from looking but I wasn't even successful at that.'' Leon looked at his hand, hesitated. The trees chit-
tered.

        ''Well, my other neighbor finally sees what's happened and
comes out. We stood there and talked. I didn't have to tell him who
did it because you could see the hemorrhage trail going across our
lawn toward Homer's place. In fact, Homer at this time comes out
of the house with some garbage to throw on his pile so he can have
an excuse to see what's going on. The barn was blocking his view.
He pretends he doesn't see us and goes back into the house. 'I
wouldn't rub him,' the neighbor tells me. Then he tells me how
Homer is crazy, how he got arrested for stabbing somebody in a bar
fight. I stood there. The snow began to fall again and was landing on
the thick fluffed hair of the collie. The neighbor went in to call the
widow whose dog it was. She lived up in the village, and I remembered seeing the kids at the store playing with it, petting it. What
happened next I'm not quite sure.'' He paused, reached in his back
pocket for a handkerchief, and wiped the sweat that beaded on his
forehead and trickled to his eyes, stinging.

        ''All I remember is seeing blood on the snow. Nothing else. I
don't even remember crossing the yard. But suddenly, there he is, in

the doorway, one hand on his hip, the other against the door jamb. I heard myself ask him what the fuck he thought he was doing. I tell him about how the kids play out by the barn and could have stepped into the line of fire. But he just leans against the door like he was in a movie and says, 'Na-unh, I looked real good.' Then he tells me how he is sick of stray dogs coming into his yard, and I say, no wonder, what with four of his own and one in heat. Then he spat past my shoulder. All I could see was the snow all splattered with blood and kids playing with the dog and when I looked into his crazy face with the mossy teeth, I had an urge to mash it into something else. He was saying, 'Any dawg what comes into my yard I kin shoot,' and I grabbed him by the shirt and told him that if he ever, ever stuck that gun out his back door again, I'd stick it up his ass and pull the trigger.''

"What did he say?'' asked Duke.

"Not much. I told him I was calling the cops and walked away. I helped the son-in-law of the widow put the dog into one of those green garbage bags, then he drove off. The only thing left was all that red stain on the snow. The afternoon was shot, literally.''

The night throbbed with frogs and crickets.

"Later on the dogs started howling. I went to the window. It was dark and snowy, but I could make out Homer, across the lot, kicking the dogs. It was a kind of animal bellow mingling with the dogyowl.''

Duke looked him in the eye, made a faintly audible sound of musing, and nodded. Leon felt they shared certain understandings and could be friends. Then he watched the eyes unwrinkle, become hard as a doll's, and close as if hidden weights had been tilted behind them. Duke looked at Sherry and pointed to his watch.

"That's right,'' said Sherry. "We told the baby-sitter we would be back in an hour or so.''

Leon said, looking at Duke, "You know, I'm not sure what my point was either. When I started to tell about Homer, it seemed I had a point. Now I don't know.''

"The point is,'' laughed Duke, "that you didn't take any shit from Homer.''

"No, no, no, it was something else.''

"Let's think about it then," said Duke. "We've really got to get back. Maybe we'll give you a ring tomorrow. We've been thinking about a day at the beach. About two hours from here, but it's always cooler. Good way to beat the heat."

Leon and Georgette nodded. It sounded great.

Then, slowly drifting toward the gate, in some nervous parting laughter, Duke turned and said, "Remember, don't call us, we'll call you."

Leon snapped off the orange patio light and foolishly hoped to extinguish as well as the heat, the noise of the swamp, the entire evening. He snugged the sliding screen wall against mosquitos and, breathing hard, looked toward the river, close by, unseen. Finally he went to the kitchen doorway and leaned and tried to think. There was the underwater rumble and clack of a few plates and glasses Georgette was washing. "What did you think of them?" she asked.

"First, what do you make of the last thing he said?"

"'Don't call us' you mean?"

Leon nodded.

"A joke . . . something to say."

"Some joke."

"It didn't sound right, but why make a mountain of it?"

"I guess."

"But what did you think of them?"

"They're interesting," said Leon. "Cool, witty. I like the way Duke talks. He's got a great voice."

"But he can't make up his mind whether he's on stage or off."

"So?"

"So he comes off kind of phony."

"It's occupational."

"It's still kind of fake."

Leon shook his head, "It's class, polish."

Georgette ran a plate under the water.

Leon said, "Hell, my whole life is fake. What's the difference? Glad-handing everyone, acting concerned, and what I'm *really* concerned about is keeping accounts and getting new ones."

Georgette said nothing; she acted as if she were totally absorbed with the forks, checking for food specks. Leon wiped his mouth and looked at the back of his sweat-shiny hand. The night made piercing noises.

"You think they were just being indulgent?" asked Leon.

"I didn't say that."

"You just don't like them then?"

"It's not a question of like or dislike. I just wish we knew them better."

Leon said, "Some people, you know, are discreet."

"Meaning?"

"Meaning they're not like you or me—they're more private; they don't spill their whole story at one sitting."

"Meaning they were afraid to be open."

Leon sighed, went into the living room, sank to the sofa. "You have a nice way of being open."

"What's that supposed to mean?"

"Why did you bring up the 'high school bad-ass' thing?"

"Come on."

"I mean it. I can't stand couples who just can't wait to let on to others that they argue or pick at each other—as if it were proof of being normal instead of screwed-up and desperate."

"But," said Georgette, bringing him back, as usual, to the point, "this teenage routine is like clockwork with you. A few drinks and you're telling about stealing cars, breaking into this and that, drag racing, gang fights, gang bangs, the whole thing. You can't resist it. You've said so yourself."

"I know."

"So what's the point?"

"I don't know."

"Some kind of nostalgia?"

Leon remained silent for a moment. "Maybe it helps me think my life has come out all right after all." He looked down at his shirt pasted to his skin, paunch-tightened, the buttons strained. "It hasn't though."

She laughed, came and sat on the sofa next to him. "Listen, don't be so serious. We get along as well as anybody."

"Sure."

"We *do.*" She leaned against him. There was affection in her look. Leon noticed a faint dew of perspiration at the roots of her blond neck-curls. "You amaze me."

"How?"

"The dog story."

"What about it?" he said, hoping she would say "Nothing" and go up to bed.

She laughed. "For one thing, you weren't reading Tolstoy."

Leon gave her a defiant look.

"Well you weren't. You were watching the football game, and you didn't go out into the yard until halftime."

"OK," he said, "OK." It was quiet. Leon looked through the window where fireflies pricked the darkness. "I just wanted to make a good impression."

"Fine. But things didn't happen that way."

"I know. That's the way they should have happened though."

The darkness throbbed. Georgette yawned and stood up. "I'm going to bed."

On the sofa, running with sweat, his skin prickled by the rough fabric, he watched her mount the narrow path of carpeted stairway, lightly, almost with a bounce. Snow slanted across the dark barn. He walked across the lot of weeds, beige stubble, past the apple tree. The house was paintless, and the back door was an incongruous bile green; it gave the impression not of having been painted in place but of having been found in the town dump and hung. He did not even have to knock. Homer was in grease-stained Levis, a checkerboard hunting shirt, black hair leaping from the dirty, torn collar of the T-shirt. He wore a demented grin, lip curling away from the bad teeth. Leon had barely uttered a word when he threw back his head and began to bark, howl like a coyote in the westerns. Black-haired, his Adam's apple bounced. As he stood sideways in the doorway, Leon noticed a brown handle showing from his hip pocket. A comb or a knife? Leon filled with rage, began to see himself bash the howling face and bad teeth. Blood spattered on the snow. But nothing happened. He stood there. Homer stepped up close and barked in his face, short taunting yips. A sour smell of beer and tooth-rot wafted from his open mouth. Leon caught a glimpse, in the kitchen, of the brother (or brother-in-law?), tall and long-jawed, at a table stacked with beer cans, the shotgun lying casually aimed at the open door. Leon began to back away, and tripped. Homer laughed and, as Leon got to his feet, he howled one last howl, and the bile green door slammed shut.

Georgette didn't know this. He was almost sure. The bile green door was his only—small relief, none really. God, it was unbearable. What could you do? His heart struggled against his ribs like a rabbit trapped in its burrow. He couldn't rid himself of the green door. Leaden, weary, confused, he climbed the stairs. In the bathroom, he lifted his arm for the light switch, and the sticky underarm and ribskin made the sound of adhesive tape slowly pulled. The mirror showed him his father's spindly hand-me-down legs, but on his father, thin, they were not absurd. If he could only do something. Through the screen came the sound of an outboard on the river. He thought of the black woman. Water would be a cool relief. Maybe not. Maybe everything stayed with you, even beneath it. Everything clung. Take a shower and in five minutes you were the same. Bachelors were lucky; when their stories dwindled, when they grew transparent, they were the first to sense it and could move on, be a bit mysterious, even to themselves. Christ, she knew him so well, too well.

With the bedroom mercifully dark, he got into bed. He lay in the heat and remembered something he read long ago about obesity being a state of mind. Unaccountably, he thought of the Greek classes of love—*eros, caritas* . . . and what were the others? He thought about the air-conditioner. At least he had not joked about the blacks. He had to relearn control. Once his father had slapped him for saying the word "nigger." He folded his arms on his chest. If he could only sleep. Things might look better in the morning. Insects ticked against the screen. Leon waited for a noise, a gunshot, something dramatic to bring down the final velvet curtain of sleep. But nothing did.

He slept in snatches and heard twice that eerie two-pitched cry. Once close enough to wake him. The second time, sleepless, he heard it far away. He wondered what it was. An owl of some sort? When it was still dark, he threw himself out of bed. Nothing was better. The painful evening with Duke and Sherry still clung. *Don't call us, we'll call you.* He went downstairs in just his tennis shorts. His ankles cracked on the stairs. It was the blue hour before sunrise. In the kitchen he put the coffeepot on the red coil. One by one the trees were coming out of the dark, their long gray beards dangling over the river. Leon drank a big glass of juice and instead of cereal and eggs, he ate a peach. He wandered about in the rich quiet, watching it get light. When he finished the peach, he looked at the red stone and noticed it was the same color as the sun just showing through the trees. The color of blood. The stubbly face, the green door.

Coffee was batting the glass dome of the pot, like brown thoughts turning to black. Cup in hand, he stepped onto the patio. A great chatter of birds came from the far end of the building. He walked around the end of the complex toward the parking lot, where another row of identical apartments, but less expensive and with no patio on the river, faced him from the other side. Car tops were already shimmered with heat. Still there were the bird cries, squawks, concentrated, as if from an aviary. Then they dwindled. The old man from the end apartment—Leon had forgotten his name—was making his way across the lot between the cars, looking about. He spotted Leon and approached. He was carrying a huge snake, arm extended from his side. Thick, almost four feet long, the snake dangled, still writhed, as he held it up for Leon's closer inspection.

"Don't worry," he said, "Ah took his hay-ud off with a hoe." Leon watched the blood drip onto the tar, become shiny and lose its color. "Hit's what we call a cottonmouth. Course you caint see the cotton 'cause the mouth and hay-ud is over yonder." He laughed proudly. "This uns a olive-black 'cause it's old. Young uns is red-brown with a black design goes like 'at." He smiled, eyes blue and narrow against the sun. He was short and wiry and had a deep tan. Leon had not yet seen him in a shirt. On his left side was that red welted scar the size of a hand and an incision line that ran diagonally across the chest. Clear blue eyes always on the move, he told Leon to tell them "gals" of his to watch where they play, not to go down by the water or along the path alone. He had often seen snakes sunning themselves. You had to be careful. Better safe than sorry. Maybe Leon would like to show the girls this snake so they would know.

"Thanks," said Leon, "I'll show them at the zoo."

Then he watched the old man walk gingerly, barefooted, over the hot tar to the big green dumpster and fling the snake into the open top. Now, suddenly, he realized that he too was without shoes and nearly jumped. He nervously searched the nearest grass and decided to enter the apartment by the sidewalk and front door. Christ, the old man had moxie, held himself well, had good muscle tone for his age. Even after that horrible surgery.

Inside, Leon put his empty cup in the sink. Again he was running with sweat but somehow didn't mind. In fact, he liked it. He gazed at the river fixed in its channel, smooth, dark, calm. Unless they had found the woman, there would be a police launch soon thrumming in the current. The house was still. He went to the closet and picked up his tennis shoes. For a moment he held them, then dropped them to the floor, and pushed the door carefully until it clicked. Sliding the patio screen, he looked once at the green phone clinging to the wall. Somehow, he knew they would never call, but it didn't much matter.

He stepped off the patio. Grass tickled his feet. He wiped sweat from his eyes, tasted salt on his tongue. Sharp. He carefully ran his eyes over the lawn before him. Birds flared here and there, strangely banded, marked. He couldn't identify them, nor most of the trees. Sunlight was on the grass like melted butter; it was horrible. Leon drew in his belly and threw back his shoulders, walked as if he were being watched. The lawn and water and sandy scar of a path that ran away from the building along the river were theatrically empty. Leon had an urge to walk, explore. He had not yet been on the path. Standing at the edge of the lawn, feeling the pressure of the sun on his bare feet, he let his eye follow the path down the embankment to a narrow brook that fed the river and could, for a start, be nicely leaped on a short run. The path climbed a long slope with tall lurking grasses at either side. Then there was a high bluff, where the path disappeared in thick bushes and emerged, lower than the bank where he stood, on a flat hook of land before the path and river swerved from view. Looking down at the dark water at his feet,

Leon imagined the black woman, open-eyed and liplessly grinning, suddenly bob to the surface, like some terrible fish. Sun pressed on his back, urged him toward the path, white as sugar and as horribly sweet. Something strange and powerful was filling his life. Slowly, he put one bare foot in front of the other, as if learning to walk again, after some long illness. Then he began to run, almost lightly.

Paper Options

Before the kid from the newspaper came by to do the interview and take photos, Hutch had checked himself out: tweed jacket, jeans, and chukka boots that looked like two large baked potatoes. A red-and-yellow hand-painted tie lay against his oxford shirt. Not bad. But it was vaguely disturbing that the jeans and boots wouldn't show in the photo. As the kid took light readings and fiddled with the window shade, Hutch tilted back in his swivel chair and gazed at his nameplate on the in-turned door; it said, in white-on-black, HUTCH. He had blackened in the DR. ROBERT and the INSON of HUTCHINSON with a felt-tip. Simplify. Less was more. Never mind the chairperson's mousey suggestions about professionalism. Hutch knew what these kids needed; they needed someone who could get down on their level, someone they could talk openly with. He hadn't been in the South for more than a few months but already had a handle on things, especially the chairperson—a gray, wrinkled, uptight guy in his late fifties. One night Hutch had entertained a few new friends by saying right out that the guy didn't know whether to scratch his watch or wind his wick. Hutch felt good about his ability to assess a situation. After all, calling Hutch "Doctor"—an obvious distancing device. Others might be cowed by the guy, but Hutch had a few things going: a book on the blocks and two articles coming out soon. Which was why this journalism major, now in his Marriage and Family course, had been sent over to do the interview. The boy's name was Thurmon. It was an off-the-

wall southern name that Hutch thought about right for anyone who
would still insist on calling him "Doctor." The distance was muddy-
ing, but the kid needed limits, was obviously afraid of rapport.
Couldn't hack it. Behavior mod took time, and it would take time to
undo all those cringing years of student as nigger. But the kid would
eventually get his thing together, Hutch reasoned. The fact was that
as hang-ups went, it was not a big hang-up.

Photos taken, Thurmon sat down and pulled out a pad. There
was something rabbity about his ears; they stood out and showed a
trace of veins. He had small, ironic eyes, an unconvincing laugh,
large red hands, and brown hair that was short, unhip. "What made
yew major in sociology?" he began.

Hutch had a flash of John Giger: he was the first prof to have a
beard at that little Methodist college of a dozen gray buildings
fastened to an Ohio cornfield. Giger—you could call him
"John"—played a nice guitar and knew Joan Baez personally.
Gave away grades. Bucked some of the old churchmen by saying
right out he was an atheist. Giger was sensitive to what was happen-
ing. Hutch loved his casual idiom. He was a real cool guy, really a
tough dude. Hutch looked past Thurman, squinted at the dim wall
to focus his mind, and outlined the appeal of his discipline, its clarity, the possibility of arriving at conclusions, precision, patterns,
progress, demythologization ———

"What's 'at?"

Patiently, Hutch explained himself, as if to a child. He spoke of a
colleague who had published a book knocking through some old accepted ideas. Dr. Baney. Well, Ed had found old plantation records
and fed the computer lots of stats on the prewar conditions of
slaves, and the computer analysis revealed that the old dusty notion
of brutality to slaves and whatnot was largely a myth. And this is
what he meant by demythologization. Really just a big word that
meant getting at the truth.

Thurmon's face was eager. "You mean, *no slaves* ——— "

"I *mean,*" said Hutch. He paused and ran his eyes over the
watery green-brown walls to the door and the nameplate. He
breathed deeply and allowed his eyes to swim back. "I mean that

some were perhaps mistreated, but myths are demolished by norms, averages, verifiable tendencies."

Thurmon bit the cap of his ballpoint, wrinkled his brow. When he spoke, his voice was a meandering nasal current: "Way-ul, I might could say on the *average* that ole Moccasin River is four foot deep. Now that don't say nothin' about that ten foot hole in the middle. And if I try to walk across on those *averages,* that'll be all she wrote."

Jesus. Hutch gave an indulgent sigh. Corn pone, just what he needed. He forced a laugh and in a good natured way tried to excuse himself by saying he didn't *entirely* agree with the book. Beside, it was historical sociology and not really his bag.

Thurmon sat there, ears twitching, and asked a few questions about graduate and undergraduate schools attended. Had Hutch taught in the South before? What were his impressions of the town, university, students? Patiently, Hutch answered, tried to be insightful, colloquial, humorous, and all the time wondered if the kid would get to his research and publications, to the co-authored article coming out shortly in *Woman's Day,* and another he did all by himself for *Family Circle.*

"Could you describe these publications?"

Finally. Hutch explained how the *Family Circle* article was about keeping a marriage going. Maintenance—that was the key word. It was about what you did when the honeymoon halo disappeared and was replaced by a ring around the bathtub. Thurmon laughed obligingly, but there was a queer light in his eyes. Southerners: polite, but unconvincing.

Hutch particularized: "Let's say you've been married a few years. By now you're into wrangling about who does what, where weekends are spent, the whole trip, you know?"

Thurmon knew, the ballpoint wiggled.

"You want to go fishing, say, and your wife likes clubs, loud rock. So, conflict is the key word here, right?"

Thurmon smiled. "Never happen."

"Why?"

"Won't never git married. I like ma freedom."

Patiently, Hutch said, "You never know, you might change your mind."

"Unh, unh," he muttered. "A lotta milk comes free nowadays, you know what I mean?"

Hutch knew. A dozen years ago he had taken to heart the same clichés of fellow workers on summer jobs: *Hey, man, stay single—different broads, come and go like you want, you got the world by the balls.* . . . Hutch had laughed at the idea that these shovel-jockeys should presume to give him advice. It was merely a coincidence, however, that he agreed with them about his freedom. But now that his status was different, he was armed with different phrases: *Love changes one's social orientation . . . Sex ends when you zip up your fly but love . . . the bachelor skims only the surface . . . the real pleasure of a child . . . giving.* . . . None of this, however, really convinced him. Nervous, again looking at the nameplate, he said, "In any case, there is this couple and they have these differences. How do they solve them?"

Thurmon laughed. "Take off."

"You think you would, but you wouldn't."

"Doan bet on it."

Thurmon didn't know when to quit. Irked, Hutch said, "Look, nobody can avoid relationships." He wanted to say that this I'm-going-to-do-my-own-thing routine was a crock of adolescent shit that one outgrew, eventually. But that would be a put-down, make the kid really hate him. So Hutch began again. "I say in the article that conflict can't be avoided, *can't.*"

Thurmon bent over his pad.

"It's there, real or potential, in marriage *or* with an Um."

"What's 'at?"

"What?"

"A Um."

"Oh, an Um or a Sleepie is, like, a word used to designate a male or female partner in an unmarried living situation. You can't use wife, right?"

"Ah guess."

"And Um isn't sexist."

Hutch looked at Thurmon, at his faint expression of disbelief. Or was this some kind of put-on? Whatever, Hutch felt like saying that the word, with any luck, would reach the South in a few years. "In any case, conflict can't be avoided."

"Gotcha."

"It can, however, be managed. This is what the article is really about. See, the relationship is like"—Hutch fished for a simile Thurmon's country heart could go with—"like pulling a hay wagon that keeps filling up with bales of hay until you get tired of pulling it. But you don't quit, hit the bars, and hook up with somebody else just because your present partner isn't helping you pull."

Hutch paused, waited for the ballpoint to stop.

"Now what that marriage, relationship needed was what I call in my article"—he said it in syllables—"a behavioral contract."

Thurmon's face seemed blank as a barn door.

"Like the couple I talked about. On two out of the four weekends, he would agree to take her out to a nightspot. She, in turn, agrees he can fish on the other two weekends a month. Each partner would forfeit his or her preferred activity if he or she violates the terms of the contract." Hutch looked at Thurmon and heard himself, as if from a distance, and felt uneasy. His phrasing somehow put him in mind of the rules for Monopoly.

Thurmon coughed. "I know I run ma mouth too much but that kind of arrangement seems kind of immature. I mean, if you *love* somebody, you don't need ——— "

Stung, Hutch interrupted. "That's adolescent romanticism. This kind of 'love' doesn't last. The question finally becomes, 'Do we discuss our problems, talk them out?' Now, I'm not saying some marriages or whatever shouldn't end, you know? People get married for the wrong reasons like sex, loneliness, security, and so on. And basic incompatibility can't be overcome.

"Which brings me to my second point: selection. Selection comes before the contract, before maintenance. Really, it's just common sense."

"Which is very uncommon," said Thurmon, scribbling, then looked up.

Uncommon. Hutch took a deep breath. Thurmon's eyes had a risible glint. Hutch saw his own knuckles go white on the chair arm. "Right, well it's also very uncommon for people to get their head together and get to know where they're coming from and where they're going. Selection means finding someone who is going the same place, with the same values and goals in mind. It means getting together with somebody who isn't hung up by your hang-ups or doesn't have the same ones. This way you can help each other. In the department counseling program I get lots of couples—students who are stacking too many roles together, you know? Parents, spouses, employees, students. It's a bummer. You've got to select well and let the contract manage the conflict, help iron out the bottlenecks. That's about it—no perfect marriages or relationships, just successful ones."

Thurmon caught up. "One more question."

"Shoot."

"Do you have a contract in your marriage?"

"Sure. If I leave my clothes lying around, if I get out of bed last and don't make it, I don't get to do what I want that day. Tennis maybe. If Anne—she's my wife—talks too long on the phone, she has to do the dishes. And the contract specifies equal responsibility for our kids."

Thurmon stood up and thanked Hutch.

Hutch said it was no sweat.

Alone, he shuffled papers into drawers until his desktop was neat, each thing in its ordered place, then found himself staring at his empty hands. With the door closed, his nameplate was gone, replaced by a black-and-yellow dartboard of concentric circles. He felt dazed. The building was fathoms deep in a disturbing, late afternoon quiet. *Do you have a contract in your marriage?* Scenes of his marriage flickered alive: images of Anne. Then Fenway and Sondra. Anne was slim, blond, and leggy; she had been his student and had gazed up at him with violet eyes as he lectured. He had published no articles yet, but she still—amazingly he thought—still loved him. Perhaps for other reasons: nine years older, he had been through Europe on a three-week tour, played a fair game of tennis, had an impressive terminology, and a wall full of books that backed him and boosted his power the way wattage does for a rock guitarist. She took him, his body like a long hook baited with phrases. They lived together, married, had Sondra and Fenway. At first, she lived through Hutch and liked it. Then: restlessness, accusations of selfishness, wisecracks about their bourgeois life-style. She disliked his friends and their "shoptalk." She wanted time to make friends of her own. Recently, after a bitter argument, she collapsed and cried until her face was ugly and glazed with tears. "I'm a fucking person too," she sobbed.

So the contract.

Hutch sat there. His mind felt numb, full—like the office—of liquid shadows that would not take flight. In the distance, between the Health and Science buildings, was a segment of the Mocassin River, which bordered the town; it was black and its banks were thick with melancholic pine and cypress. There was no point in remaining any longer at the office; no students, nobody to talk to. There were certain uncertainties, and the old Piranesi stairway made him hurry for the bright yellow light beyond the swinging doors of the first floor.

He felt sure that his emotional coloring came from the old Victorian building, but outside he was quickly wrapped in humid blankets of heat and felt worse. A sick yellow sunlight lay thick in the grass. And there was some kind of flower along the campus walks—another horrible yellow. Hutch unchained his bike. Christ, by the time he made it home, his shirt would be sweated to his back. Hutch didn't like the bike, he liked the idea of the bike and of Hutch gliding along and seen by students. *Why did you major in sociology?* Thurmon, those twitching ears. Hutch wondered how the photo would print, tried to imagine his expression, the beard and rimless glasses (once in a newspaper photo the lenses had blanked like heliographs and made him, he thought, look like an asshole). And what about the bookshelf? The bookspines—would they show clear or muddy titles? Which authors would show?

By the Sigma Nu house, someone yelled "Hutch" from the tree-shaded porch of white Doric pillars. Hutch waved blindly. A girl in a white bikini ran across the street, her breasts nicely heaving, and joined her friends on a patchwork of blankets. This rock music that beat the space between buildings, those tanned bodies, the couple leaning against the tree with arms hooked about neck and waist and staring into each other's eyes, the green outburst of leaves—Hutch hardly knew whether all this illustrated his thoughts or stole them. Thurmon's "love." Hutch knew it well because he and Anne had lived it: sunbathing, the pool, bikes. An excitement now gone. Whatever it was they had, had fought for and shed tears for, written mad summer letters for, that wild gentle thing—love, sex, need, whatever it was—was gone. And with it that sense that everything was important: the veins of a leaf, a gumwrapper, whatever. Gone. But perhaps just as well. All the worry, jealousy, sweated periods, the moony, grab-ass time you wasted when you could have been getting a handle on things.

Hutch coasted along River Road that was flanked by trees and ran like a dull double of the curving shiny black surface beside it. Recent rain had made the water very high and fast. *What do you think of the South?* Hutch didn't think he would ever get used to the bugs, mosquitos, heat, humidity. And snakes. The river was full of them, mocassins. The river was rightly named all right. Hutch hated it, the gloomy trees, the din of birds, the glossy flow; it meant nothing, had nothing to do with him, his way of getting a handle on things. And it posed a threat to Fenway and Sondra. But Anne flipped her hair back and laughed, laughed in that annoying way, probably just to burn him. She said it was a Poe scene, gothic, far-out. Sometimes it seemed between that first summer and now, nothing had happened. But not so. They had Fenway and Sondra. Everything was different. Anne was no longer impressed, argued with his views, recently had said—in front of friends—he didn't know shit. Conflict, you couldn't avoid it. Their marriage wasn't perfect but, thanks to the contract, it was successful. Unlike Thurmon, Hutch knew that life meant more than just doing your own thing. You had to be realistic about things. His shadow slid along the unpainted boards of a high slat fence that circled the apartment complex. He swung into the parking lot around an island of tall boxwoods, saw Lam's van parked next to his Vega wagon.

And swung out again.

Christ! That black van with those hand-painted gas-blue flames—it banged him into a snit. He was in no mood for Lam and Tena. Lam was in the art department and into van art. Probably for the extra bucks. It was deep-dish mags, low profiles with big white letters, Plexiglass tear windows, sun-roof, and all kinds of shag inside. Yeah. Lam liked to be visible—good for business.

Hutch pedaled along River Road where it was jungle on both sides. Maybe they would leave. His spine prickled. Lam was a drag. He was second-generation Cuban, dark, skinny, and caved in about something that had been removed by surgery. He wore a vicious scar on his olive chest, a gold chain around his neck. *Misterioso.* He allowed you to believe he was dying. Maybe to make you feel sorry and be less critical of the drip paintings he did—paintings so fucking simple it was absurd. Hutch was convinced that little Sondra's drawings and watercolors were far better. At least Sondra could draw. But what rankled Hutch was Lam's titles. One painting—it was half-blank, half-drippings—was entitled "Thesis/Synthesis." Not really knowing Lam at the time, Hutch had said a few words about Hegel and dialectics and color struggle. Lam shot a look at Tena, and they began to cackle. Lam said the titles were a put-on for certain gallery types who would stand there holding their chins and do a verbal jerk-off over some phrase copped from some philosophy book. Hutch pedaled. Sweat stung his eyes. He could see Lam on the living room floor, slouched against the sofa, in his knapsack, hair in a long ponytail cinched with a red rubber band, eyes glassy and smirking. Lam was all *laissez faire* but Tena. . . .

Tena was into another trip altogether. Hutch could see her, too, braless, with her bold saucer eyes, sitting sideways in the lounger, her legs dangling as she spoke of a favorite subject: herself. She had been a Spanish major and was more in love with the idea of having people hear her speak Spanish with Lam than she was with Lam himself. She often told how she threw away a Fulbright because she would never be a political pawn. She had been fucked over enough, especially by her straight, well-to-do Milwaukee parents—parents she regularly cursed for having messed up her head. No more. Now she had her shit together. She was into her own thing, and her own thing often involved leaving her little girl, Genesta, with "friends" for long periods of time. Hutch could care less that her Spanish asides to Lam went over his head (language nowadays was bullshit, was the way he saw it: everybody spoke English and anything worth reading was translated), but he *could* care about her aggressive tone, her presumption, the way her thing often threatened yours. Recently, trying to get Hutch and Anne to open their marriage, Tena told how last summer, camping in the Baja, she got balled in the van by some other guy. Lam watched and dug it. Without being told, Hutch had a sense of where Genesta was, felt that—even though all the data and stats weren't in yet—felt that the experience, for a child, might not be positive. Lam laughed. He said that the guy had loaned them some water, was *muy simpatico,* and the whole thing was really beautiful. The validity of Hutch's observations depended on objectivity, but Lam's behavior seemed backed by cynicism and that let you off the hook, too easily. On the other hand, it was very clear to Hutch that Lam was a casualty of the war and the antiwar movement because now that those things were only a memory, Lam was left with little more than the goofy threads, hair, beads, and bitterness. It was clear all right. Drifting was Lam's defense (this was his third job in four years), and "open" was his and Tena's magic word. Anything closed was bad. Gut was good. But these little bromides meant little to Hutch and try as he might, he found it difficult to drift, to smoke dope more than occasionally, and Lam's grassy idleness was finally a bit maddening, unproductive as hours and hours of adolescent kissy-kissy. But Hutch did smoke, on occasion, just to be sociable, to let Lam and Tena know that their thing was OK, but not necessarily his.

Hutch coasted into the parking lot again. The black van baked in the unreasonable sun. That was it. His shirt was pasted to the skin, and he wasn't going to bike around like an asshole for another minute. He leaned his bike against the slatted fence that enclosed their patio and slid back the screenwall, which cried out for oil. Joint smoke twisted into his nostrils, acid rock batted his ears. They were—as he had foreseen—slumped on the floor amid strewn album covers, Tena sideways in the lounger. Up came Lam's raspy, stoned voice: "Hey, man, fall down and get wasted."

Hutch placed his chukka boots between the sprawled legs and stepped over.

"New bong," said Lam. It sat in the middle of the floor. Amber plastic. It was the size of an exhaust pipe with two clear tubes curving back from the brass bowl into the six inches of water in the bottom.

"Try it," urged Tena. There was an edge to her voice.

Anne watched, anxiety in her eyes.

"Nice cool smoke," tempted Lam.

"Be *sociable*." They laughed, slow spaced-out laughter.

Tena said, "Por favor, no es la muerte."

Anne echoed, "Si, es la tienda de frutas."

And they laughed again.

Hutch said, "Cut the shit, talk English."

Lam said, "Hey, amigo, dunt you comes to May-he-co wis us?" It was his Alphonso Bedoya number.

Hutch said, "Hey, I heard you were taking some psych courses."

Lam said, "You heard that?"

"Right, somebody told me you wanted to get your head on straight."

"No, man, I hear you taking a Spanish course."

"Right," said Tena. "You're coming to Mexico with us."

Anne giggled, "Si, con nosotros."

Hutch gave her a black look and said, "No way."

They moaned, then laughed.

Hutch sat on the edge of the sofa. "Shit, Mexican jails are full of turkeys like you."

Tena said, "Not us, we got our shit together."

Lam lit the bong and lifted it up to Hutch.

"Not right now."

Tena said, "Come on, be *sociable*."

They all giggled again—some kind of private joke.

Lam said, "Look at it this way. You get out of jail in Mexico, and you got no record in the States."

"Hey, that's a good way of looking at it," said Hutch and tapped the knapsack. "What's that, your stash?"

"Un hunh, Castenada, man, he's got it all together."
"Great."
Stalemated. It was just an act they went through. Hutch left the room. Lam cackled softly.

He changed into a dry shirt and jeans. In his book-lined study, he slumped into the swivel chair and tilted back. This chair and the one in his office were almost the only places he felt comfortable lately. Especially the latter. With the door open and students passing in the hall, waving, saying his name, or stopping to chat, he felt good. The chair somehow promised objectivity, as long as he remained in it. Giger used to say that participant observation was, for many in the discipline, fraught with risk, and Hutch learned painfully that he was right. Smoking dope and becoming intimate with students—well, for Hutch, it was very clearly a way of going native that darkened the waters. Coeds were too dangerously pretty and, more than once, Hutch had lost his handle on things and was nearly swept away.

He looked out the window. The building had two wings that created a courtyard where each apartment had a few brick stairs and a sliding glass wall, which opened a family life to scrutiny when the curtains were not drawn. Perfect for observation. And Hutch enjoyed watching. As an observer, he saw himself the equal of a good novelist. He had a way of assessing other people, summing up, keynoting their qualities.

Randy, a short thick graduate student, marched between the two tall brickwork gate-posts in the fourth wall of the courtyard. Randy had on his red football jersey with the number 69 and was carrying a bat and an orange baseball glove. He did his porky walk up to the sliding glass, where his wife, Jolene, floated in white. Hutch's observation of Randy and Jolene had played a part in his forthcoming article in *Family Circle*. They had too many roles, too little money. Hutch knew there was tension over the second car, a Jaguar, which Randy, an average good ol' boy, sprinted about town in with one of his fraternity buddies, rebel-yelling and nursing a can of crotch-warmed beer. Being a mother, student, and wife was too much for Jolene. She often haunted the window with a wine glass in her hand. Hutch saw into their lives with absolute clarity. But their problems, of course, were familiar, the pattern predictable. A business major, Randy would never be able to do anything but make money and neglect his family. Neglect—rich fathers as well as poor were guilty of this, and the stats and cases that fattened his files at the office proved it. It was a real bummer. Hutch watched them drift, like fish, into the dark behind the glass wall. Systems of agreement, contracts—these were what had to replace infatuation and the initial selflessness of a relationship. Had to.

Hutch grew restless. He walked from room to room, restricted to the upstairs, as if he were under some kind of house arrest. From the children's bedroom, he looked down on the gaudy van next to his own unconvincing Vega wagon. Maturing meant accepting dullness. Or did it? Who said that? Hutch listened irritably to the loud rock surging up the stairwell. He went back to his study, the hollow-core door clicked behind him, but still he was pricked by the music and the loud snatches of conversation that drifted up with it: "Heav-vy!" "Listen, listen." "Can you dig it?" "Me gusta mucho." "Oh wow!"

Sondra appeared in the courtyard. She was in white shorts and a yellow jersey and from this height seemed very small, vulnerable. Her hair seemed white in the sun. Nate was behind her on the sidewalk; he wore an orange shirt and his crippled arm was stiffened at a slight angle from the body. He had white hair, long, trimmed youthfully. Sondra was laughing wildly. Nate made faces and drunkenly lunged after her. Hutch frowned.

Nate was a real trip. Retired, he drank to protect himself from boredom while his wife—she was younger and attractive and had a tennis tan—taught at a distant branch campus. A few weeks ago, when Hutch was here at his desk, both trying to get a handle on things and mind the children, he suddenly became aware of a third voice downstairs, a man's voice. He bolted at the intrusion and bounded down the stairs and there, in the den, sprawled on the floor in the clutter of dolls and tinker toys, round head tugging on its thin stalk of a neck, was Nate, laughing, the whites of his eyes taking over completely at times. Sensing Hutch above him, he revolved his head and slurred, "We's having a ball." And the kids laughed, seemed oblivious to the fact that something was wrong with him, that he had crashed their apartment, that he was unable to find his feet without Hutch helping him. Then, flopped on the sofa, he smoked sloppily while Hutch helplessly watched the ash lengthen and fall to the carpet. Nate mumbled about how much Fenway and Sondra were a part of his life now, how their visits to his apartment made his day. Then he gargled on about his son, A. J., who had been shacking up for a week now, about how he wanted to get out of this cow town and into a city where a body could really cut loose. Oh yeah! Ten, fifteen, twenty minutes, half an hour—Hutch thought he would never leave. Nate was becoming harder to take. Drunk, he would blather on, making terrible inroads on your time—time better used to sort out and focus. And Hutch wondered, finally, what sort of games were keeping Fenway and Sondra in Nate's apartment so long on sunny days when they should be outside. But when he asked them, they were annoyingly vague. Anne said, "Jesus Christ, cool it. You're impossible. What do you think, they're having an orgy or something?"

Hutch replied calmly that Nate was a case, that last week, alone, in the middle of the courtyard, he was whirling a big chain: vroom, vroom, vroom. "That's normal?"

Blithely, Anne said, "Maybe that's his thing."

Hutch didn't argue—that's one thing he didn't do. Hassles were a failure of reason, a loss of control. Yelling never solved anything, he reasoned. The purpose of contractual relationships was to reduce, eliminate outbursts. Nate and his wife were a case in point: you could hear them arguing viciously when the windows were open at night. His wife was brighter, more reasonable and should have been able to negotiate certain things with Nate. If he persisted in getting fried, she should have certain paper options. Hutch wondered why so many bright people made a mess of their lives. He would take it upon himself to become friendly with her, invite her to play some tennis, and talk about his research and writing in such a way that the point would be made. She was bright, had lovely lips, ash-blond hair, nice tan limbs.

A screen door screeched in another world. Hutch became aware of the courtyard: empty. Through the pulsing rock, he heard Nate's voice, its volume boosted by booze; the voice was asking to take Sondra for a walk along the river to feed the ducks. Hutch went into the hallway. Nate would never notice that they were toking up. Hutch went into the children's room and looked down on Nate and Sondra who were in the patio, directly below. They were two heads with arms and toes. Then they elongated, grew to different sizes, and went through the gate of the fenced-in parking lot. Nate held her hand as they crossed a down-sloping field toward a wall of trees that hid the river. Hutch watched them enter the bushes. Nate stumbled once, and his orange shirt went into green. Hutch stared at the slanting trees. Suddenly the window framed an emptiness. His throat clenched. He wished Lam and Tena were gone. Where was little Fenway? He wanted to have a talk with Anne.

The doorbell rang, and Hutch came down the stairs. Anne was telling a little red-haired boy, Fenway's playmate, that he was probably out in the back. She closed the door. Hutch repeated the little boy's question. "He's out back, OK?" She was defensively annoyed, but her tone was spacey and had a way of mocking trust. Her eyes, in the dimness, were dark blank pools. A wildness took him, and he felt like taking her head in his hands and banging it off the wall, but she was already back in the den, and Hutch took his frightening impulse into the dizzy sunlight.

Fenway was at the end of the building. Looking lost, he clutched a ragdoll with a pull-cord that set off an eerie recording: "Hello . . . My name is Miss-us Mee-ber and *I* want to be *your* friend. . . ." Hutch squatted and said into Fenway's face, "Don't you follow Daddy, you go back to Mommy, OK?" Fenway stared, remained mute, and yanked the pull-cord again.

Hutch ran along the path bordered by high grasses toward the river. Everything burned in the slow, late afternoon fire, and Hutch was glad to reach the dimness of trees. It was quiet. He puffed to a stop at the water and tried to decide which way they went. Downstream the trees were thicker and the verticals were crosshatched with deadfalls not yet touching the ground. Hutch turned upstream, and as soon as he rounded the bend in the path, he saw Nate and Sondra. They were playing some game, laughing. Hutch announced himself by yelling, "Hey, wait for me." Nate swung around and swayed. He grabbed his belt and hoisted his tan trousers, which were too large and cinched about his waist in gathers.

Hutch caught up.

Nate reached him a hand the size of a shovel. "Well nah," he said, continuing to pump Hutch's hand—one of his endless snapping turtle numbers that could go on until sunset. "Wasn't no need to bother."

"I know," said Hutch. The bones in his fingers ached.

"I take good care of this little gal, don't I?" he said, nodding to Sondra.

"Sho do," she sang. Hutch seethed. *Sho do* had been added to *reckon, fixin to,* and a few other nit-witted southernisms she had already acquired. She said, "Why did *you* have to come? *We* always have a good time."

Hutch laughed. "Well, I can see I'm not wanted."

Nate let go of his hand.

They sauntered on. Nate repeated. "I love this little gal."

"Sure, I know you do."

"She makes my day."

"And you make hers," said Hutch. The litany was familiar, irksome. Shreds of Nate's sour-mash breath drifted past his nose. To Hutch it was an odor that spoke of weakness and defeat and waste. Especially waste. Hutch's discipline required reasons. There were always reasons. Perhaps he could get a handle on it. Hutch asked about Nate's retirement.

"Oh yeah," he replied vaguely.

"How long?"

"Couple years. You writin' a book?"

Hutch laughed; he felt like telling about the *Family Circle* article, but he knew that Nate would be as unappreciative as Lam and Tena, whose response to the several offprints he had given them was never more than a few words of faint praise. "No, I just thought that since your wife teaches at the university, you could take some courses for nothing."

Nate stopped, pulled at his trousers, and laughed. "Nah, not me. I'm havin' a ball." Pronounced *bowel.* "I go fishin', I"—he lunged, catching his toe on an exposed root—"I git drunk, read."

"What do you read?"

Nate turned: his eyes were crooked and long, pink, like the splits in late tomatoes. Hutch couldn't read them. "A little of this, a little of that."

They walked above the fast black water. Nate said, "Know when the Magna Carta was signed?"

Hutch didn't. "Fifteenth century, I guess."

"June 15, 1215. . . . Know where at?"

Hutch didn't.

"Runnymede," said Nate and let the silence lengthen. "Yeah, always liked history."

Leaves and twigs sped past on the flat broken sheen of the surface. Sondra skipped ahead on the path that was now angling higher above the water. Nate stopped and hitched up his trousers so that the white wool socks and penny loafers momentarily showed under the cuffs before the waist slid back to its usual place, just below the little paunch that tightened his orange shirt. Hutch began to notice that his cheek sometimes jerked, flickered like a neon with a short. "Naw, I'm readin' this book about prisons. Know what pressin' was?"

Hutch didn't, and this quiz number was getting on his wick.

"Put a guy under a door with spikes and add weight ever day 'til he dies." Nate laughed to himself; it sounded like water running from a tub.

"Nice," said Hutch.

"Come on," Sondra called from further up the path. She was finding sticks and running to the edge of the high bank and throwing them into the water, for the splash. Hutch was growing nervous. He called to her, "Wait, Sondra, and hold Daddy's hand."

"No!"

"Sondra!"

She turned and did a lip-fart, adding, "No way."

Nate said, "Yeah, I've always liked to read."

"That's great," said Hutch. Sondra scampered off. She found

more sticks and flung them into the sweeping current.

"Learn a lot from readin'," lectured Nate.

"You ought to read some sociology, psychology."

"Psychology," he repeated. "Know what they says about life?"

Hutch said nothing.

"Says it's like a Co'Cola bottle."

Nate's cheek flickered. Hutch stared. And thought: *What is this, Zen or something?* "How's that?"

"Today it's in your hand and"—Nate paused and smirked—"and tomorra it's up your ass!" And he coughed out a rachety string of laughs. He repeated the line and clapped Hutch on the back.

Sondra danced ahead on the leafed-over path that now curved along the riverline. In yellow and white, dappled by a low sun, she taunted, begged for a smack, but Hutch knew that psychologically it was not good to punish a child before others. A submerged branch, snagged by something underwater, made a ripping sound. "Sondra, honey, please come here."

"I don't want to."

"Nate, where are these ducks?"

"Up yonder," he said vaguely, annoyingly.

Hutch rolled his eyes upward. Nate was really off the wall.

"See, they move with the pickins."

Hutch pushed a branch with bell-shaped blossoms; it snapped back.

"Like ma boy, A. J.," said Nate. He paused, patted his orange-shirted paunch. "He been shackin' up with some college gal for a month now."

"Does it bother you?" asked Hutch. He sensed a sexual jealousy that was rather common now, generational.

Nate said, "I tell him to get all the ass he can and don't never get married."

Hutch bridled. "But you did."

"Nah." He gurgled.

"I mean *you* got married."

But Nate was lost in the river. He said, "I got this"—with his good hand he tapped the stiffened arm—"as soon as we hit the beaches. I was 16th Infantry, First Division. Normandy . . .''

"No, I mean —— "

He looked at Hutch, a greedy light in his eye. " . . . and I was ready for some voolay voo cooshay . . . half hour . . . bingo, a mortar got me. . . . "

Sondra had a big unwieldy stick. "Sondra —— "

"I don't *want* to."

Nate adjusted his pants for the fiftieth time. A dirty white rowboat with a small droning motor made slow progress against the current. An old black man sat in the low stern with one hand on the motor that churned up amber-black scarves of water. The tip of a fishing rod quivered over the prow. Nate said, "He probably been fishin' gar. You got you a mess of gar in here."

But Hutch didn't give a shit about gar; he was more interested in Nate as an alienated ex-GI and was beginning to get a handle on the wound, the source of Nate's whole boozy trip. "Were you bitter about that arm when you came back to the States?"

"Oh yeah, won't nobody but a nigger eat a gar." He looked thoughtfully at the river. "Even the Indians had nigger slaves."

Hutch bit his lip.

"It's a fact. Cherokees." Nate inhaled with some kind of odd pleasure. "Oh yeah, I love to read. Wife's the one watches the tube all night. And she's a teacher." He snorted. "Not me. I read this book about the Indian wars. Now a lotta folks like to say it was all peace and harmony before the white man come." He fixed Hutch with his pink, crooked eyes. "No sir. They's killin' each other by the thousands. All kinds of tortures. Take a guy naked and stand 'im on a stake, a sharp stake just a little up his rectum so's he caint git off . . . bleed . . . get weak . . . sinks on it til the point touches his heart."

"Lovely."

"I read about another one where. . . . "

Hutch thought about the pointed stake and the Coke bottle. It wasn't really a pattern, but Nate had some kind of funny anal thing, some kind of mutilation fantasy. He wasn't really into sadism except in his unconscious fantasy life, like everyone else, so there was no social danger. But a little Q and A still might lay bare a paradigm, a syndrome, might uncover factual data that would support his notion that Nate's drinking thing was a ploy to bury the trauma of mutilation and shell shock. Hutch almost moaned with pleasure. The idea, born that moment, already shimmered with certainty. The wounded are obsessed with wounds—hence the sharpened stake and the Coke bottle. If Nate could only see his problem, talk it through with somebody like Hutch, he might change. But Nate was a trip. He was defensive, evasive, and, as such, unhelpable. But what really threw Hutch into a snit was that people like Nate posed unthinkable problems to social engineering.

"Sondra, come here I said."

This time she simply laughed and ran ahead.

Nate said, clapping his huge hand on Hutch's shoulder, "Me and you've got a lot in common."

Incredulous, Hutch heard himself repeat, "In common."

"Oh yeah, we just need the basics"—he gurgled and elbowed Hutch—"a little booze and a little poontang." He wavered near the path edge. It was too close, and Hutch grabbed him by the arm.

Out of sight, Sondra yelled: "DADDY!"

And Hutch ran ahead. Around the bend, he saw her standing in the middle of the bare trail, holding a box turtle, and watching him run toward her. Then she screamed. Hutch saw the crack grow in a swift zigzag, the earth open. Tree-crowns fell as if, by dozens, they had been simultaneously chain-sawed. Looking at him, Sondra slanted away, her mouth shaping a soundless scream. Head down, Hutch saw his feet planted in blue. Everything blackened, chilled. He writhed and broke water, gasping and spitting. His mouth burned and yelled for help. Already he had been swept far. Sondra and Nate were still on the bank, shrinking, then pulled back around the bend. Hutch was a weak swimmer and felt his heart in a squeeze of panic. The chukka boots were like flatirons, and he went under again. The force against his eyeballs made images stutter in frames of light. It could have been the beginning of death: the moment lengthened, as it did when you bonged up on good stuff. He expected some voice from a shaft of sunlight, a rerun of his life, but saw only his nameplate, HUTCH, and a jumble of words and phrases: SELECTION, HANG-UP, FAMILY CIRCLE, DATA INPUT, OFF-THE-

WALL, and others. They spun, as if in a slot machine. Thurmon's face smirked fleetingly. It was amazing how long it took when you expected to die. But it was air again—air mixed with swampy water, and he gagged. Still moving fast, he felt more buoyant and realized the chukka boots were gone. Glasses too. The world was blurred. There was a bouncing swatch of orange far upstream. Hutch, his clothing binding, foundered, stroked clumsily for the passing bank that, he now saw, had been deeply undermined by the fast high water. Roots, snakelike, dangled temptingly; they begged to be handled, but Hutch knew he risked pulling a ton of overhang upon himself. He threshed and tried to touch bottom, but the current was too strong. A great wreck of a tree was coming upon him; it was bleached, the limbs stumped and nubbed; it was somehow anchored a few feet from the steep bank. Hutch caught it, strained, and threw his leg over the trunk. Only now did he realize how exhausted he was. He gasped, coughed, puked: the yellow patch stretched and snapped away. "You OK down there?" Hutch looked up and squinted: an orange blob. Hutch couldn't believe that Nate was already there. Couldn't believe. He wanted to tell him to watch Sondra, and he would find his own way out, but Nate was already reaching him a long branch. Sondra appeared beside Nate, looking down, still clutching the bag of bread crumbs for the unfound ducks, and crying. Nate pushed her back from the rim. The limb waited. Hutch flopped, kicked, and grabbed it. Nate grunted, "I gotcha." And he did. With one good arm he held and the two red, quivering faces contemplated each other as Hutch came over the top.

The foul-smelling water drained slowly from his short sleeves, dripped from his long hair, nosetip, and beard. He tugged at his plastered clothing to smooth out the bunches, looked down at the white splotches that were his feet.

"Shook that ol' tree loose," said Nate.

And Hutch squinted at the black watery vista where the old white tree-body was quickly being swept away.

The screenwall screamed. She was yelling, "Daddy fell in the river," when he pulled back the drapes and stepped into the room, giving off mud-stink. He went into the kitchen and rummaged

about in a drawer, finally finding his old glasses. The room flickered
grayly from the TV, sound turned down. Lam was on the floor,
leaning against the sofa with his arm around Anne. Tena was
slouched, still sideways in the lounger, nodding to the heavy moog
and pulsing beat—something by the Grateful Dead. They were
laughing softly, almost pretending not to notice him. He wondered
if they had dropped acid, but it was just a blissful trippiness, the
usual. Fenway sat in the hallway with his ragdoll; it was saying,
"I'm Miss-us Mee-ber. . . ." Like an owl, Lam finally swiveled his
head. "Hey, man, far-out."

Tena said, "Oh, qué mala suerte!"

Hutch stared at Lam and Anne. He thought about Tena's Mexican number last summer, about Lam always saying that jealousy
was bourgeois. Lam canted his head upward; in his pupils were discs
the color of butter. He chuckled. "Bum trip, man. The gods are trying to tell you something. Read Castenada, get wasted, and listen to
the spirits and forces."

Hutch looked at Tena. She measured him with her large bold
eyes; her expression spat at him for being into a will power trip. But
it didn't matter. He wanted to get the black leechy water off his
flesh. He flung his arms, flicked his hands, and watched their
mouths form words he couldn't hear.

He showered and told himself what had happened. The riverbank
was undermined; he had fallen in the river. It was simple. But the
black water, thick and quiet as oil, flickered its footage in his mind,
and he toweled off briskly, as if trying to rub it away. Anne breezed
into the room. She put her hands on her hips and sarcastically told
him he was really cool. It was as if she were saying it from a TV
screen with the sound turned down low. She was trying to tell him he
had fucking freaked out, slinging that muddy water on them. What
was the idea? She turned and looked at him in the bureau mirror,
where he wavered in its dim depth and could barely make himself
out. Frightened, he put on his shirt.

She lifted a hairbrush. "All Lam wants to do is get you out of
your head."

He pulled on his shorts. He didn't answer.

Dragging the brush through her hair, looking at herself in the mirror, she muttered, "You got to get out of that jive trip. Lam says you're always laying this heavy shit on people. *Proposals, funding,* and all this *data* shit. Lam says. . . ."

Hutch couldn't talk; he felt the river in his throat. Suddenly it seemed as if he were in another bedroom with someone he had hooked in a bar. He watched her slip out of her jeans and experienced a faint quickening: guilt and sexual longing.

"Your terms are all *ab-stract,* imperial. Lam says you should read Castenada, you know? Go through illusion."

Lam. The name began to chase a numbness from his mind. But somehow he did not want to speak. He searched for trousers, pushed a few empty hangers, and stood listening to their sad music. He walked to the bathroom. She sat in her panties, her foot hiked on the edge of the tub, shaving her legs. There was a honey-colored stain at her crotch, a faint one, and a few black glossy hairs hooking around the elastic. She looked up and laughed, a stoned giggle. "Why don't you want to come to Mexico with us?"

May-he-co. An imitation of an imitation: Lam's. Hutch had plenty of reasons for not wanting to go, but what was the point of trotting them out? He belted his trousers, turned about the room, and sank to the edge of the bed, looking out the window. Nate was limping across the quadrangle. He gestured to Jolene and Randy. His mouth moved silently. They laughed. From the bathroom, Anne asked, "What are you afraid of?"

He got up and walked to the bathroom doorway, feeling he ought to answer but sensing at the same time a deep frightening indifference until he heard her say *Lam says* and discovered himself shouting that he didn't give a fuck what Lam said. About anything. His speech came as a reflex, almost like swimming: "Lam is a loser and his wife is an opportunist. You know, one of Lam's colleagues told me he has never had a show. Guess why?"

"The Establishment"—she was addressing her legs—"is against him."

"Establishment shit!"

The razor scraped, a hollow plastic sound.

"Whatever you say." She closed her eyes and snorted.

Hutch hammered the door with his fist; it banged against the wall.
Her eyes popped open. But she collected herself, stood up, and
opened the mirror door of the medicine cabinet, and, for a moment,
he saw himself in his old, orange-framed, plastic glasses that didn't
fit his beard, glasses he wore long ago as an undergraduate before he
————. But she slammed the door, aborted his thought, and pushed
past him into the bedroom. Dental floss whirred on its spool. She sat
on the edge of the bed and flossed her teeth with the help of a make-
up mirror that magnified her gums. There was a twang and snap.
The quadrangle was empty, green, full of tricky shadows. Downstairs, in the deep stillness, he heard Fenway's doll: "My name
is. . . ." The floss did its last snap and twang. Anne looked up. She
was still in panties. Her mouth opened; it said, "You wanna ball?"
Hutch felt no softness for her. His hands, he knew, would be lying.
It would be wooden: a plank and a nail.
     She laughed. "See, Lam's right—you're into a head trip."

He lay down on the sofa in the living room. With the old glasses,
things were a bit indistinct, watery, menacing. In the children's
playroom he heard, "I'm Miss-us Mee-ber and *I* want to be your
friend." It was insistent but remote. When he closed his eyes, it was
black water, the acid choking, his nameplate spinning, Thurmon's
smirk, the dangling snakelike roots—everything spun in the whirlpool of his fatigue. Anne's footsteps sounded on the stairs. Her hair
was combed out long and glossy, and she had on a bright green peasant blouse with red and yellow hand-stitched flowers. He asked
where she was going.
     "Out."
     "Out?"
     "Yeah, out." She looked down and let out a grassy giggle. "You
know who cleaned up the mud and shit you tracked in?"
     He knew.
     "Me. You know what the contract says about the floors?"
     He knew.
     "And you know what that means?"
     He knew, he finally knew.
     "Where are you going?"

She turned for the hallway. He called to her back, "Are you going to Lam and Tena's?"

She didn't answer.

"You going to let him *ball* you?"

He heard the screen door slide open with a painful shriek. Fenway cried; he wanted to go with Mommy. Anne said no: "You be a good boy for Daddy." The door shrieked again.

The evening sky, through the window, had gone gray; it looked old except for a mysterious streak of lavendar and pink over the trees by the river. He became aware of Sondra; she stood by his side, clutching her Raggedy Ann with its big black eyes, bright red hair, and isosceles nose. In the river he saw nothing significant: his nameplate and an absurd flotsam of words. Fenway sat crosslegged in the middle of the floor. Sullenly he pulled the string: "My name is. . . ." He had blond hair in a Dutchboy cut, pixie face bones, the sweetness of a destroying angel. Hutch called him. The boy came. Sondra said, "Daddy?"

"What?"

"I'm sorry."

"For what?"

She put her dimpled hand on his chest. Tears glanced down her cheeks, and as she leaned over him, he saw himself going under in the dark water of her eyes. He sat up quickly and took the children in his arms and held them and held them. Sondra rested her head below his chin. "I love you, Daddy." Her sadness was as real as the terrible dark current of the river, more real than anything Hutch had experienced in months. "Sondra, I ——— " He spoke slowly, tentatively, like a man taking his first exploratory steps in a familiar darkened house where the furniture drifts but doesn't and often surprises in excruciating ways. "I know," he said, "I know you do." And hugging them more tightly added, weakly, as if it were an impossible promise, "Daddy loves you too."

Black Water, White Ducks

Wendy felt better in the kitchen, alone, by the mullioned windows that looked on a segment of the river. But the apartment was hot, and there was no sanctuary from the cigarette smoke. She had to put them out of mind—her mother and father, Hank and Teri, and the TV roaring with football. Her mother was grayer and more wrinkled and just sat there with a drink in one hand and a cigarette in the other.

Wendy stared at the river and leaned against the sink. For months she had been safe. Now this visit from her parents. And the letter from Cass, her old roommate, lay in the bedroom begging response. And she had sketches, preliminaries that begged to be paintings. The night class was a looming menace and. . . . Cass had an almost cruel way of making you think yourself a failure.

The narrow fast river made Wendy uneasy. Little Teri could tumble in. And there were snakes. But most of all, the ducks were gone, and darkness was closing with its late November speed and the leaning cypress seemed ready to fall in the river. *Let yourself go with the fast current*—it's what she felt like doing after the ducks disappeared, a white flotilla that some wonderful loony old woman—she lived in one of the down-river condominiums—had bought a few months ago. They were so preciously white in a landscape dying for color. But they constantly quacked for handouts, and the quacking must have made somebody complain to the manager. For a week now they were gone. But they had left their voices, and Wendy at odd times thought she heard them and went to the window to see—nothing but a thin blade of light on the black. . . .

Water boiled on the stove, and Wendy removed the pot from the red coil. Eating—they would be eating again. A sour taste haunted her mouth, as if her digestive tract were backing up, as the plumbing did when the river rose after heavy rains. Teri kept asking where the ducks were. And Wendy hated the question because they were gone, simply gone, and she couldn't do a damn thing about it and wished Teri would stop asking that question and give her some peace and quiet. Teri could just go play a game, make believe they were there.

"Quack, quack." She wondered if she had actually made the noise. But who would notice? Hank, Teri, her mother and father were buffered by other noise in the den, the sunken room she had for months proudly wanted her parents to see: the stone fireplace and the sense of space created by the big glass wall and the way the cereal-colored carpet and the dead grass outside ran into one another and seemed to marry. But her parents said little. Three full baths, tile, sauna, huge bedrooms, the wrought-iron balcony overlooking the river, the Spanish moss that they, as New Yorkers, had never seen before—none of it fazed them.

The fierce red coil seemed to pulse. She hit the switch and watched it fade. The ducks were gone. At night you couldn't any longer see their reassuring white bodies huddled on the bank, glowing. And that letter from Cass—it should go into the fire Hank was keeping. He rose, thunked another log on the snapping fire, and sank deeply into the arms of his favorite chair, deeply, so that it seemed to engulf him. He gave a sigh of satisfaction and the fingers of his right hand curled about the glass of Wild Turkey. Wendy cranked out one of the windows over the sink. From the refrigerator she took carrots, potatoes, onions, and radishes and set them on her cutting board. Football, as if muffled by cotton, thumped and roared. Her father was veiled in smoke. His eyes were pouched and baffled as he sat, belly in his lap, a smouldering butt between his forked yellow fingers. Her mother had Teri in her lap now. Wendy wanted to look but couldn't. Teri climbed right up close to that rouge mouth-hole, the slablike cheeks and wattles, as if there was nothing horrible about it, about the neck ruts and the way her chub lips left smeary crescents on cups, glasses, and obscene red bands on butted cigarettes. No, instead Teri said, after one of their crazy games, "Oh, gramma, I love you." Then the frighteningly predictable: her mother's laughing face and slitted eyes, a thrown-back head and a wide-open mouth full of big teeth like the horse in Picasso's *Guernica,* the laugh a kind of soft nicker. The air was lethal with smoke yet Teri sat with them, even snuggled, and allowed herself to be hugged half to death. It was crazy and with her parents smoking, Hank had a carte blanche, a curving dark pipe set between his small teeth and thin mulberry lips. He puffed with a kind of sleepy contentment. In bed, he would not smell of flesh—he would smell of smoke. Wendy had married smoke, garlands of it. Her clothes were tainted by it. Rituals of fire and smoke. She thought of church, candles.

It rankled: her mother insisting on driving across the railroad tracks to the black section of town for Mass—the only Catholic Mass for miles around, a Mass flavored with Baptist *amens* and *hallelujahs.* The thought of it—all those unpainted, tin-roofed shacks standing on cinder blocks, sagging porches, the clapboard church with its dwarf steeple, Father Dacey with his usual sermon about injustice and the poor—the thought depressed her, put her in mind of Cass and some of their shared moments: protest marches, white nights of discussion about the war, the role of the church, their roles. But in this church, she felt out of place, and went only occasionally. Father Dacey was ———. The church had none of the old jeweled-cave darkness. Windows were of clear glass. Floors were wooden, and if you put a marble in the aisle, it would speed toward the altar and veer madly to the left. And Father Dacey never gave literary sermons or mentioned Donne, Camus, or read from *Le Petit Prince* as the young priest at the Newman Center had when she and Cass were students. This Father Dacey somehow put her in a terrible mood. But what would she say when her mother squinted and screwed up her mouth—as surely she would—and asked about Teri's religious training?

Quack. Maybe that's what she would say. Maybe she would dredge the past for material, then tell her off, beat her with her own tactic. Tell her she looked like Albright's *Ida.* Wendy had an impulse to utter burning words, let herself go, but she had already—to teachers, college president, hawks—and it wasn't worth it: adolescent folly. Besides, her mother might just avoid the subject of Teri's religious training. She had so far, and they were leaving tomorrow. Wendy was baffled. Sometimes she was astonished by her own behavior. What had happened on the day they arrived last week showed her that in spite of self-study reading, she could still meet herself as a stranger, a total stranger.

At the airport, waiting for her parents, she was pure expectation, plans for the week. A honey-colored sun poured on the pines and tobacco barns and cypress knees and made them more picturesque than ever. But her parents didn't notice, looked at the flat moving landscape as if it were as familiar as the hills of upstate New York, and began to bicker at each other because of something that happened on the plane. Then her mother swerved the argument to include Wendy and why Aunt Theresa hadn't yet received a thank-you note for that darling little dress—an expensive Carter—she had been nice enough to, thoughtful enough ———.

Enough, enough! Wendy screamed and banged her white fists against the wheel. Tears rivered, the road blurred. *I-can't-take-it! You drive me crazy! I look forward to seeing you and . . . what? This shit! Always at one another.*

The memory ached. She shouldn't have reacted that way, frightened them, but it just happened. And worried about her, they were forced to a truce. For almost ten miles. Then they argued about whose fault it was that Wendy was upset, so she screamed again and intentionally swerved the car down a small embankment and into a ditch. A red-and-white Marlboro billboard loomed in the windshield. She ran into the woods, sank against a tree, and watched her father puff up a short knoll after her. Somehow it seemed distant and almost laughable now, like one of the anecdotes Cass might have told six or seven years ago. But Cass had become, in her letters, very serious, and nothing was funny anymore. She would love to see Cass but that might only worsen things.

The kitchen was hot, and the window was a grayness framed. No quacks, no white smears on the river, nothing but the dark flowing, smooth and blackly quiet as draining crankcase oil. Cass was into karate and wrote that it was important to be able to defend yourself. From what? Wendy choked the ground meat stuffing; it oozed and dangled from the webs of her fingers. She turned the tap and washed her hands in a braid of slow water. Washed them thoroughly. She recalled a magazine story where a young man talks about his aging parents, their travels, insights, feelings about age, and sees them as fearless explorers in the wilderness of Time. How lovely. Teri was flicking the lighter for her grandpa who had another butt tucked into the corner of his mouth. And her mother: *No, heavens no,* she had said when Wendy proposed a few days on one of the islands off the coast: fresh salty air, flour-white beaches and glossy breakers, tennis, *fruits de mer.* But her mother closed her eyes, shook her head, puckered her lips, and said: *No, heavens no. That would be crazy for your father and I. That kind of place is for ritzy people.* Wendy's face flamed, acid rose in her throat. How could anyone have such a fixed notion of who they were? This was partially why she did not want to invite any friends to meet them. She wasn't ashamed, she told herself. Her parents simply didn't care, at their age, to meet new people. And her father (a barber with mouse-colored hair—a listener by trade) would remain mute, his fretful fingers opening and closing, as if clipping an invisible head.

Tomorrow they would leave. She did love them, but it was just as well. Her mother had already exhausted deaths, divorces, marriages, and scandals. And if any friends did drop in, it was certain her mother would drag out an adventureless girlhood, the Great Depression, or tell harmless but unfunny jokes about Catholics, Protestants, and Jews. Terrifying. Wendy held the knife as if protecting herself from a street assailant, then began peeling and cutting potatoes. Then onions. Something within her fell to its knees. "Dear Jesus, please. . . ."

Hank came into the kitchen for another dose of Wild Turkey and noticed her tears. His face sharpened with concern, and when she held up the onion, he laughed with relief. The freezer opened, cubes rattled from the automatic maker, clinked in the glass. "Hey, hey, hey." Hank had been saying that for years. An idiotic souvenir from his med school fraternity. He was bearish and had an old sack of dead food for a belly. She watched him lumber to the sunken den, amazed at her ignorance of him. He sighed back into his chair. *Peace means absence of thought: thinking means saying no.* Where did that come from? Sometimes she was sure it applied to Hank because he never read. And she never stopped. But he could say sharp things, casually, good-ol'-boy style, and show you that there *was* something going on behind those slow green eyes: "I don't know Cass as well as you and I ain't no genius but this assertiveness training thing—I mean, anybody who's got to take a course to learn how to be rude. . . ."

And rude he wasn't, not even aggressive, and liked to mock himself in front of others, which galled her. *Hank's the name, jawbone's the game.* An oral surgeon calling himself just a fancy mechanic, just country folks. Like his commonsensical uncle who, a simple farmer, could cure any ailing pig or cow in the county. Hank told her she was more talented than Cass would ever be. Or himself for that matter. There was the design of the new house and the interior of this apartment with her own wall hangings, pottery, and paintings. But she had a "crabby" disposition and if he couldn't joke her out of it, he could make her a mouthpiece to keep her, a nightgrinder, from breaking her fillings. "Crabby" was his version of endearment and affection; he was mad for nicknames. She watched him puff himself, Saturdays, into local identification. Football. Not even a year in this town and he was calling himself a "Tiger" and really seemed to care about the team. Last year, before they moved, he had been "Purple Panther." And he was genuinely depressed when "we" lost. But he had a passion for work, could focus, hum, and lose himself. Practical, like Cass.

There was a roar, a yammering voice, cowbells, drums. And her father told him he just missed a helluva play. But of course he didn't because the replay came hotly after. Like falling back into the same nightmare you had just awakened from. "Hey, hey, hey!" Teri was tugging at her skirt for something to eat. Giblets sizzled in the dim light, and the coil, like a small red planet, slid into view. She stood there and couldn't recall moving her hand. In a tone of wonderment, the announcer called it a thing of beauty, that block, dexterity and timing that even Heifetz would envy. "Ask your father," she hissed, squeezing Teri's sticklike arm. Teri began to cry. Wendy scooped up her purse, snatched her coat from the hall closet, and went out the front door to the parking lot. Hank's face hung like a pale balloon in the black gap of the doorway. "Where are you going?"

"I have to get a few things at the store."

Drink in hand, he offered to go, as if his leaving the game were actually possible. She fished in her purse, in a chaos of junk, for the keys. Where *was* she going?

She was going to spin out of the parking lot in her birthday Triumph. A neighbor was jogging in a blue warm-up suit. He waved, face handsome, a ruddy straining smile. And turning through the handsome suburban streets near the apartment, she saw other runners, men and women. Their numbers were growing. So many these days. All those punishing miles. And with such regularity you could tell the time. Like her mother with Mass, novenas, First Fridays. Hank wouldn't understand because he had the office and hospital for protection, helped people, and was never so happy as when his Motorola pageboy, clipped to his hip, squawked at a dinner party or during a quiet evening so he could jump up and run to the Emergency Room in her Triumph. But even if he was at home, he couldn't, as she once believed, stand between herself and—she couldn't name what it was.

She stared into the windshield; a pair of animal eyes ignited by the lights shot back to the dark. But away from that sentimental fire, it was nice and cool. She drove aimlessly, simply glad to be alone and in possession. It was a good feeling, almost as good as the moment she left Teri at Park-A-Tot. *I am only able to live when my mind and fancy are completely free.* Tow-mahss Mahnn—that's the way Cass said it.

A runner loomed into the headlights, his face a fierce red mask. There was the front campus of old brick, the huge magnolias and Van Gogh cypresses writhing into starlight. It was all deserted but for one or two of the art faculty who were working in their studios behind the big white squares of light. Mr. Keith, her Advanced Drawing instructor, had eyes that went right through you, spoke little outside of class, and worked endlessly with turbulent colors, menacing landscapes. He was recently divorced and encouraging of her work—sketches of a huge tree hulk on the riverbank. The bone-white root system made a fantastic skein in the black water. Huge and dead, it had been there for years and had a kind of permanence. She was in awe of its hard, smooth, barkless durable body.

She found herself passing Park-A-Tot with its candy-striped play equipment. With Teri gone, she often played tennis and learned where her muscles were. She felt a child again, the body both big and small, dark, a good place to hide. The after-ache was good, gave you moments of true feeling, stood between you and . . . moods. Cass had once written her about sentiment and false feeling. Cass had a way, almost cruel, of putting things. Her letters subtly revived memories of shared interests, differences, implied Wendy was a sell-out. Wendy could almost hear that lockjawed voice: *Giving means giving yourself away. Family sentiment kills, becomes your career. Where does it end?* Wendy thought of the ditch, the Marlboro bill-board, her mother screaming, and the trees rocking. The letter con-cluded: *Glad you're happy—not all of us are so lucky.* Should it end here? Wendy thought. No. It was fake misery, a hip costume, and Wendy wanted to write and tell her so. From Tow-mahss Mahnn to position papers to the Low Rent scene. How terrible. Friends, they scarcely knew one another.

In the store, she held the wine bottle by the neck and wandered in the aisles. In the appliance section, the ranges reminded her of the red coil—was it on at home? Hank would be happy; it would give him a chance to tell her fondly how spacey and scattered she was. It was a role she was supposed to inhabit. But she had plans for him: "Hey, hey, hey," she would sneer at him, tomorrow perhaps, when they went to the new house again with her parents to check the pro-gress and Hank's good saw would be there rusting in the framework of studs.

Wendy lifted a warm-up suit from the rack, a black one with large white stripes down the legs. White. Like the ducks but the sight of them vanished as she looked at cheap suits the color of Spanish moss. In the dressing room, she kicked off her shoes, unbuttoned her skirt that fell and pooled about her feet. She removed the rest of her clothing until she stood in bra and panties. The mirror gave her a large close self. Her breasts were round and had a gourdlike fullness, but they were not too big and would never be a problem. Even Hank said that. And her hair was long and glossy and full of light. She stooped and removed a small compact mirror from her purse. With her back to the mirror and using the compact, she lifted the hair to the top of her head: a nice long neck and curving, knuckled spine, lovely. But loveliness ended with her bottom and thighbacks that were slightly dimpled and needed certain exercises. In the sweat suit, she was happier—it was a tangible promise—and the sour taste in her mouth had fled. Her eyes gleamed. She smiled and looked at herself in different moods, over her shoulder like a model. Closely she studied her face for lines. Her smile vanished. She looked again and saw her mother's features, in hiding all these years, faintly, then more harshly, sketch themselves about her eyes, mouth, cheeks, and chin.

She drove around. On days when it rained, when she couldn't paint, couldn't find a tennis partner, she drove around like this; but it wasn't dark as now, and she would look at old, tin-sheathed tobacco barns as if they were paintings. She would drive past shacks on brickwork stilts, clotheslines drooping and a-flap with laundry; past fields where bandanaed blacks, faces polished with sweat, stooped, or leaned on hoes; past wallows where black-and-white Hampshire hogs stood looking like old cast-off saddle shoes, big and bloated. She knew these country roads by heart. Familiar odors, fences, and farms came like answered prayers that calmed her less and less. On the radio, a preacher yelled in a deep cracking voice about Jesus and getting saved. *Saved*—simple as the past tense. Your worries were over. The voice worked itself into a kind of nervous breakdown. Other voices encouraged: "Oh yeah!" "Praise the Lord!" "A-men!" Finally, on the other side of nervous collapse, calm, the preacher asked the listeners if they loved Jesus and wanted to be saved. "Jest tell Jee-zuz what you want. . . ." Wendy wanted the ducks back in the river. But the preacher grew manic again, and it reminded her of Sister Gertrude in the seventh grade and those bloody pictures of Christ Crucified, "holy pictures," you got if you were good. But Sister was most often depressive, and one day she had big glass tears rolling down her starched-in face, and the rowdy boys laughed while she cradled the big statue of the Sacred Heart and rocked it back and forth saying, "We won't even listen to them, will we?" Phil Gumbo's ugly face laughed, snorted, twisted itself. The spectacle of Sister weeping took Wendy by the heart and made her sorry. Angry.

Looming pines that flanked the car rolled to a halt on Forest Hills Road—a fresh slab of macadam that snaked through the tall columnar pines past a few sites where new homes were being built. Rows of 2 × 4 studs made a skeleton that glowed in the dark. When Hank wasn't at the office, or hospital, he was here. It relaxed him, he said. And he had his beeper in case he was needed. And his pipe. And his red hunting vest. He was well-organized. Hank thought of everything. He wasn't scattered like Wendy. Sitting in the Triumph, she smiled at her plan and rehearsed the moment in her head: *How in the world? Hank, your saw—it's all rusty. You must have forgotten it. And the square too! You're getting so spacey! Ah do declare! It must be from living with me.* So good natured, he wouldn't even hit her. Just laugh like an idiot instead. *Hey, hey, hey.* With the pipe stuck in his face, he would hide his head in a pillow of smoke. On the radio the preacher said to touch the radio and pray. Wendy imagined hundreds of hands, arthritic, white-spotted, phthisic hands trembling toward the glowing dials of old radios in farm kitchens and rooms of inescapable dust and darkness. She snapped on the flashlight, took the square and saw from the trunk, and walked through the mud toward the frame of their new house.

The TV flickered. Wendy felt restless but nicely anonymous. Dinner had gone well, with Hank taking care of the finishing touches like sauces and dressing and wine. Wendy endured no odd looks, exploratory comments. Hank and her father were still treating her gingerly, treating themselves with drink and were blurred and chuckly, absorbed in a whodunnit. They all smoked. The room stank. Wendy sat by the doorway in the rocker, but smoke still took the back of her throat in its scratchy grip. In the usual way, her mother was cough-laughing at the silly commercials. "My heavens, all you have

to do is take a bath, wash your neck once in a while . . . Slobs . . .
Who could ever need such a powerful soap?'' And Hank laughed
wildly, as if he never heard her say such things.

Then they tried to solve the crime. A police doctor, young and defiant, was convinced of homicide. His older partner was uncertain.
Wendy's mother guessed suicide and trotted out the reasons. Her
father, naturally, disagreed. Hank laughed at the hospital scenes,
the fakery. Suspects doubled, suspicions wavered. Finally the older
doctor proved the death was natural: hardening of the arteries. But
nobody guessed it because the victim was so young. Hank cackled.
Wendy tried to rock away her nervous legs. In an upbeat Epilogue,
which finally wasn't very upbeat, the young doctor brought a gift to
his uncle at an old folks home. There was a freeze-frame of him
smiling on a long porch of terminal rockers. Wendy jumped from
her chair and went to the kitchen. Her mother hissed. Wendy peered
through the darkened window. Her mother, seldom wrong about
the outcome of such programs, seemed testy when she said good
night. And later, through the vent that somehow connected the
guest room and kitchen, Wendy heard her mother's furious
whisper; she was telling her father that Teri was all skin and bones
and ate too much candy and too little dinner. And, as if predicting
the outcome of a cheap TV drama, she said that no good would
come of this: ''You mark my words and see.''

Zipped into the warm-up suit with white leg stripes, she sat on the
front stairs to lace her Adidas. The street, when she closed the front
door, was empty. Only one curbed car the whole length. There were
blank facades where a few lights, here and there, came to the windows, pressing, as if wanting out. An abandoned bicycle lay lonely
in the grass. The neighborhood plaza was deserted, shops shuttered.
The moon shed a bony light, and shadows were horribly elongated.
It was like running down the street of a De Chirico. Her steps were
heavy, gluey when she heard a thick breathing at her back. There
was another shadow. Wendy glanced quickly. A hooded figure, a
woman's face, familiar, flushed. There were little strangulated
cries. She quickened her pace, but the dark figure matched her stride
for stride.

She woke up, sitting, and in the bureau mirror a self revealed itself, open-mouthed, like *The Scream* by Munch.

Hank was gone.

Her body had a terrible odor. She needed a hot shower that might bring her warmth as well. There had been too many icy farewells. The scream had to be stifled but not replaced with its bored echo, the yawn. Her parents deserved neither, said an inner voice, almost her own.

The shower warmed and soothed, but when she came into the kitchen so washed with sunshine that the scrambled eggs and orange juice were almost invisible and everyone oddly shadowed and momentarily quiet, as when a stranger enters an already intimate group, Wendy was afraid she would say or do the wrong thing. But her father affectionately teased her about sleeping late and Hank said, "Hey, we've been up for hours."

Or if not hours, thought Wendy, looking at the mist of smoke in the air, at least long enough to fill that big ashtray. But speech wouldn't come. Not even something friendly. Like her father's compliment to Hank: "Hank here fixed it all!" The reasonable voice she heard in the bedroom fell silent, silent as her mother who said nothing, who was looking for attention she had every right to, for at a certain point the child must be a parent to the parent. Wendy listened to the voice and chanced a question: "Sleep well, Mom?" She watched her mother's spoon dive into the sugarbowl: *chuff.* Then a tinkling sound as the coffee churned into a small tan whirlpool that went horribly around and around until Wendy felt herself on the verge of drowning.

"Yes," said Mom, looking up and smiling. "I slept fine. Did you?"

"Like a log," said her father.

"Not you," said Mom, and gave him an elbow.

They laughed. Her father was forking eggs as if he were stoking their old furnace. Wendy felt a lift. The light helped; it slanted and arranged and picked out her parents' faces, lit them perfectly, and she saw they had that ruddy flush you saw in a portrait by Hals. Round peasant faces with merry eyes that coincided with what she saw or imagined at the moment. And their faces grew more precious as Wendy realized they could be portraits seen for the last time.

Teri said, "Gramma, *you said* you would tell me about when you were a little girl."

Ah, this was a tale her mother never tired of telling—The Great Depression, selling apples, terrible winters, snitching coal from passing trains. But the phone rang. Hank scraped back his chair. Talk stopped. "I'm on my way," he said to the phone and hung up. Then the goodbyes to her parents. "In case I'm not back. Car wreck. This sounds like a bad one."

"Oh, don't you worry about a thing," said Mom. "We'll manage just fine."

And they did. Teri sat in the back with her grandparents and listened to the things they did as children. "We were very poor when I was a little girl and our house wasn't as nice as yours but I was happy because my mother and father loved me." The rearview held her mother's face, heavy, hazed with bluish smoke, the eyes puffy and sentimental and moist. She took a deep drag on her cigarette as if trying to pull back into herself all of the things that were gone. Wendy wanted to say that nothing vanished entirely, that one could make oneself this or that, but at the first hint of philosophy or corrective suggestion, her mother would freeze up. No, that wouldn't work. Only the old routines and reminiscences, the loving and elaborate talk about nothing would soothe her and save the day. So that when they passed the billboard and ditch where she had run off the road, nobody even noticed and when the awkward hugs, kisses, and goodbyes were accomplished in the terminal and the silver plane leapt into the air, became cruciform, grew small, and disappeared into its invisible and scarcely believable path, Wendy could not quite contain herself; the sadness and grief were sudden, surprising her like a muscle cramp. As they drove from the terminal and the Carolina pines fled backward, she could still see her father support her mother as she shuffled on painfully swollen feet and ankles. When she had hold of the railing, he took her pocketbook, switched position, and took her left arm to help her up the long slow stairs into the plane. The dark yawn of the doorway finally took them and the door was closed, sealed. There was a moment of deathlike quiet;

then the engines whined. Wendy tried to find her Mom's face at one of the windows but couldn't. God.

"Mommy?"

"What?"

"Why are you crying?"

Wendy drove with one hand. She dried her cheeks with her fingers and the back of her hand. "I'm just sad."

"Why?"

"I'm just sad to see Grandma and Grandpa leave. Now don't *you* start too"—Wendy noticed her mouth set and the chin whiten and dimple—"or we'll be in a terrible fix!" Their stricken faces made each other laugh. "We'll go to a show this afternoon, OK?" *Show*—God, that's what her mother called them. And she used them in the same way: as cheerups. Mom took her everywhere, gave her everything. Wendy was the center of her life until—and even after—she grew up and went away to school. A few months ago, on the phone, Wendy asked what she was doing. The reply: "Just sitting." And Wendy knew it was true. Her mother's life was a crime that could not be undone. Not now.

Teri said in a hopeful voice, "But we going to see Gramma and Granpa in the spring, hunh?"

"Yes, we are."

Teri was quiet. She was standing in the back seat, her head just off Wendy's right shoulder. The sun flickered in the trees. An old white-haired black man on a tractor was making furrows in a field.

"Mommy?"

"What?"

"People get sick when they get old, don't they?"

"Many of them do."

"But Gramma Butler isn't sick."

"Grandma Butler takes care of herself. She's active. And she doesn't smoke." Her tone was harsh. Teri was quiet and the quiet accused. "But Grandma Butler is lucky too. Everyone ages differently."

"Will Gramma be active if I, ah, pray to God."

"I don't know, sweetheart."

"Mommy?"

"What?"

"Mommy, will you ever get like Gramma?"

"I don't know! Please don't ask Mommy so many questions."

The road flew under the station wagon. Tin-sheathed tobacco barns flashed in the sun and trees washed by them. Wendy stiffened as a big semi came at them and went by with a shaking *voom*. "Dear Jesus, please," she whispered.

"Mommy?"

"Please! Why can't you just ask Mommy the question?"

"Mommy?"

"*What,* sweetheart?"

"Mommy, we're going more than the sign says."

It was true—they were going 70, but Wendy didn't want to be told how to drive by her child. Then she saw a state trooper and quickly dropped her speed. She felt criminal.

And only slightly less criminal at the new house. She left Teri in the station wagon and tried to skirt the mud, gingerly picking her way from dry spot to dry spot past the pallets of bricks, plywood, studs, and other building materials. She climbed into the house and retrieved the saw and square she planted yesterday. Wendy was not Cass—she knew that. She had her own role to play, and it didn't involve faddish politics or being fashionably unhappy. Unhappiness came soon enough—you didn't have to work at it. But Cass had been important to her and there was still a certain gratitude. *Thinking makes you superior to your fate,* Cass once quoted. And Wendy was thinking. She stared at the teeth of the saw. The letter would stay in the drawer. She would not reply. She had other things to think about. The ducks, for instance. They were not gone entirely. She would get to work, put them back with paint, huddle them on the bank of a midnight river under a shaving of moon and the suggestion of leaning cypress.

Teri called. And Wendy hopped from island to dry island, lightly, laughing her way back, the square in one hand, the saw on the other. She remembered buying them for Hank: his birthday. And he had another one coming up soon. That to think of as well. Before setting the tools in the tire well under the decking, she wiped them with a rag.There was only a thin coat of rust, and it came off as easily as a mist of Windex. Seeing them shine again, she felt more buoyant than she had in a long time. She paused, took a deep breath, and looked at the tall pines and the sun winking in them. It was quiet, very quiet, and far off a church bell sounded, and she felt a deep and sudden freshness within herself. Against all odds.

Private Flights

Zig drove with one hand, yawned violently, and pumped down more black coffee. God, shaking sleep was hard these days. But it shouldn't be, not this early in the afternoon. He worked less and made more—much more—than he had as a reporter. A step up. But he no longer had stories to hold his interest; nowadays his interest was most often feigned so that he knew the real thing when he felt it, and the last few sentences of the three o'clock news straightened him as if a leg muscle were starting to cramp. He tried to find another station, but the radio produced only rock music and a manic preacher. A Gulf sign grew in the windshield, and he swung from traffic.

The mechanic wore a red hunting cap and blue overalls with a bright orange Gulf at the pocket. "What news?"

Zig mentioned Coach Ryan.

His thick eyebrows jumped in surprise. "Ax them kids inside. Fill up?"

Inside, in the sharp smell of kerosene, Zig listened to one of the teenagers, stridently at odds with the rock music, say: "The plane was caught in a electrical storm. . . . He's missing, presumed killed."

Presumed killed. It was painfully odd that the boy reproduced wire service language almost exactly, instead of using his own speech. Zig buttoned his coat. Bruised clouds bunched across a low sky. First time in his three years in the South it had been so cold. He shivered, nosed his car into traffic. Coach William "Red" Ryan.

Only thirty-four. Ten years younger than himself. Victories and winning seasons. Winning personality as well. Eyes black and merry, full of sparks. At the Stadium Club, Zig had pumped his hand a number of times, and Red, when he detected Odette's accent, jokingly trotted out some GI French. *Presumed killed.* Zig experienced in a more piercing way the loss he felt after the last postgame show: it was announced that Red Ryan would be taking a new post with one of the Big Ten schools. Odette upstairs asleep, Zig sat with his bourbon and stared. The Sunday night postgame show was a ritual but, with Chris now away at college, it was one he observed alone. *Presumed killed.* And Ryan's career just taking off. Zig wondered about his own. In some circles, this new job was certainly an advance. Maybe it was. You had to move. One of his old college buddies greeted all change with: *Yessir, all part of growin' up!* A bright, funny jock. Like Red Ryan. An interview with Red was always more than the standard I-feel-like-that-we-was-up-for-it-and-played-real-good. Red, in private, did mock interviews. Once at the station, after a taping session, he did an imitation of the coach at Eastern State and had everybody in the studio laughing. Zig would miss seeing him around town and on the screen enjoying himself, laughing. Zig no longer did. Maybe that was it.

Parking the car, he could see Duncan rocking on his heels behind the plate glass of Sound Heaven. Duncan was losing his hair and looked like Broderick Crawford; he wore a dark blazer with a clownish yellow tie. Zig had an urge to drive away, but Duncan spotted him and beckoned him in. God. He had no heart for it, not today, but there he was, standing on the springy green shag with red splotches that always made him think he was sinking into a garden salad. Some kids were trying out a quad system and the sound was deafening. Duncan pointed with his chin toward the back, and they moved out of the noise a bit. Speaking out of the side of his mouth as if he were giving out a tip on a longshot, he said, "Hear about the coach?"

Zig nodded.

"Shame," he said, looking at the green shag, "terrible shame." His bereaved expression suggested a mask bought in a novelty store.

Then another expression: eyes shifty, cheeks and mouth working.
"But doesn't it strike you as funny?"

"What?"

"That plane flew off course across three states and passed directly over us before it crashed in the ocean."

Zig could find nothing to say.

"*I'd* say that was fishy."

Fishy. A word Zig recalled Duncan using one afternoon in connection with his own elaborate theory of the Kennedy assassination. Wasn't it *fishy* that Oswald. . . . Something about Cuban labor and the Japanese electronics industry.

"I mean, do you know why the coach left?"

"Sure. For a better job."

Duncan smirked, slitted his eyes. "I heard he was high-handed with certain people."

"Certain people?"

Duncan nodded.

"Who?"

Duncan swiveled his eyes. "University president."

"High-handed?"

Duncan nodded.

"How? High-handed how?"

"Well, it's not important." Meaning it was; and Duncan's information was classified.

"What does all this have to do with the crash?"

"Nothing maybe. Just irregularities about the sports program. But hey, I've got a hunch the coach bailed out, parachuted into a new life somewhere." He laughed. "A while ago there was a TV movie about a guy setting things up so he disappeared and started over again in Europe. New I.D. and all. I've thought about it myself"—he laughed again—"but I'm flying high right now."

"But the coach ———— "

"I know, I know. Hey, let's forget it," he said, as if Zig had brought it up. "A good man has gone to his reward." His face got that look of cheap sorrow again; the eyes fuzzed, then brightened, and Zig watched the coach's shadow disappear as simply as if a light

switch had been thrown in a dim room. But the light was too bright.
"Listen, I got a couple of new concepts I wanna hit you with."
Concepts. Zig winced. He had introduced the idea of local merchants doing their own commercials to the station manager, and the idea took off. Duncan and others were afire with it, enjoyed seeing themselves on TV, and said business improved.

"Ready?"

Zig nodded and tried to move away from his beery breath.

"How's this for a concept? I'm sitting in a Lay-Z-Boy with my headphones on, OK?" He flashed an experimental smile. "Tuner, turntable—everything on the modular shelves behind me, OK? I've got this blissful look on my face. Now, you ready?"

"Ready."

"Now this lovely thing—my daughter-in-law—twitches by me in slow motion. She's wearing something, you know, that reveals the merchandise (wink). Now I'm so far into music heaven, I don't even bat an eye! *Fan*-tastic, huh?"

Zig coughed.

"Listen, concept number two. We get a couple hundred new dollar bills, OK? I hate to use fake money. Anyway, we get a couple of knock-out sorority girls. . . ."

We? Zig gazed past Duncan's shoulder toward the wall of TV screens, which just now featured Coach Ryan's still photo in black and white and in various shades of color. He was smiling; there were laugh lines at the eyes. Some of the screens were blackened, like nagging squares of unfinished crossword puzzles that Zig labored over and finally discarded.

" . . . and they'll be on their knees throwing all that money up in the air, the air full of fluttering sale savings." His grin widened. "Huh? Sell it with money and a little sex! Whataya think?"

"First is better."

"Sure. I *knew* you'd like it. Listen, Zig"—Duncan glanced at his watch—"I've got to see a man about a horse." He winked. "Who've you got in tonight's game?"

Zig was still staring at the wall of TV screens. "Sorry."

"Tonight's game—who've you got?"

"Ah . . . Who's playing?"

Duncan gave out a little bark of a laugh; his slabby cheeks bounced. "You look tired. You need a little strange stuff." He made a pumping gesture and laughed. It was irksome, someone like Duncan telling him how he felt, what he needed. "Virginia and North Carolina is who's playing."

"I'll go with Virginia."

"Don't bet on it." Duncan shook his head and smiled wisely. "Two of their starters won't start."

"Really."

"Injured." Again the know-it-all smile. "You won't read that in the paper though." He looked around to make sure his comments were not being monitored. "We'll work out the details for a taping session next week, OK?"

"Fine."

He winked. "Gotta see a man."

See the bottom of a glass was more like it, thought Zig as he drove away from Sound Heaven. But a few jars wouldn't be a bad idea, especially on a day like today. *See a man.* Every day was a detective story. Zig found himself driving along the river in a cold foggy light that reminded him of what clouds were like when you cut through them in an aircraft and lurched in the turbulence, your stomach on the rise as you watch the wings flex and fantasize them shearing away from the fuselage.

MARINA RESTAURANT AND LOUNGE. Zig sat at the bar and looked at the boats rocking on their reflections; nothing was leaving the harbor. Spook, in his white shirt with rolled-up sleeves, limped back and forth on the duckboards. "Hey, har yew? Usual?"

Zig nodded. There were several other men staring at the end of a soap opera. Spook shined a glass, then poured. "What's happenin'?"

"Not much. How about you?" He hoped Spook would say something about Red Ryan, his face etched with sorrow and wonder.

Spook said, "One you did fuh the Garden Center about wanna keel me with laughin'. Bobby Joe all got up like Mother Nature, jumpin' out the tree"—he slapped his thigh and hunched over—"Now that about kilt me!"

Zig said thanks. He sipped his drink to the echo of what Spook had said, how he said it. The local idiom and accent came alive again for the first time in ages. Out at the end of the pier was a dark cut-out of a man, half-lost in fog, leaning on a spile. Closer, to the right, were two white boats on their muddy low-tide sides.

"That Jenny Price stee-yul wukkin' fuh Channel 8?"

Zig said yes, she was on vacation.

Spook winked. "She right good to look at." He limped off toward another customer. The plate glass dimmed. The figure at the end of the pier was gone.

The news was about to start. On the screen was Billy Hedgecock; he was beaming, saying: "Buy a Buick, you'll never be sorry." Zig flinched and looked away. The first item on the local news wasn't local at all. It was about the fifty-two American hostages being held in Iran. Followed by the story of a local woman, eighty-five, beaten to death by two teenagers for $11.25. God. Zig downed his drink and raised a finger to Spook. Finally the screen held the coach's face and a tacky background drawing of a plane with broken wings and the unnecessary caption: CRASH. Karen Towson, still with a cold, read from her script in a distracted way: " . . . on a recruiting trip and it was to have been a routine one-hour flight to Birmingham, Alabama. The two-engine private plane took off at 9:10 P.M. and ran into a violent thunderstorm en route and radioed for a new course. They were instructed to climb to 21,000 feet and maintain their heading. But radar showed the plane slowly climbing to 25,000 feet, when it made an unscheduled turn to the northeast. There was no subsequent radio contact and thus began a four-hour, 1,000-mile odyssey that ended when the plane crashed into the ocean more than 100 miles off the coast of Virginia. Two Air Force F4 Phantoms made visual contact with the aircraft over North Carolina, but other forms of communication failed. The plane by this time had reached an altitude of 40,000 feet. The Coast Guard is conducting a search that has been hampered due to high seas. The cause of the crash may forever remain a mystery. The plane was owned by Medley Construction Company of Dallas, Texas."

The pier outside was gone. Darkness pressed at the windows. Zig sipped his drink. The image of that plane above moonlit canyons and dizzy gorges of cloud, alone in all that space, wouldn't let go. Zig had seen those deep gorges many times and stiffened slightly each time the plane, big or small, began its descent through clouds. You jounced about. Metal groaned. Deathlike faces looked at you. With the cloudscape gone, windows blanked, and a faint odor present, the pilot's voice crackled into being on the cabin speaker, reassuring, telling passengers to remain seated with seatbelts fastened. Once, a reporter in Cleveland, Zig was on a flight into Lakeside; the plane began its descent from sunlight and, almost as if reading his desire, the pilot took the plane back above the clouds. It happened twice more and just when the passengers began looking at each other, the intercom came on: "This is the captain speaking. You may have noticed a Piper Tripacer off our left wingtip. Well, the pilot's having a little difficulty, and we're trying to help him find his way home. We will be landing shortly at Lakeside." And they did, but without the Tripacer. Zig recalled it vividly—he wrote the story. A novice pilot and his girl friend were pleasure flying from Akron to Cleveland. A front sped in from the lake. They climbed above it, but the pilot realized too late he didn't have enough fuel to outrun the storm. Three times the pilot of Zig's plane tried to bring him in on his tail. Each time panic made the Tripacer climb for the sun. Finally alone above the clouds, gas gone, they began their plunge into the lake. Many times his mind, as it did now, produced a picture of that doomed Tripacer, tiny, alone above the clouds, in all that inhuman space.

God. That was long ago. The incident flashed to mind almost every time Zig flew. And he flew often. He signaled Spook. This would be his last—he didn't want to get lurchy, didn't want to meet one of the wise-guy reporters and have him say, "Hey, Zig, you're zaggin' a bit."

"Lightning got um."

"Way-yul, ever man is entitled to their opinion."

The bar seemed to change dimensions. With the windows blanked out, the place seemed smaller, the men on the other side of the horseshoe closer, more intimate. A boozy illusion. They sat on another planet. He had talked with them in London and Paris, in pubs and cafés. Being a mate meant simply being there, and better if you had been born there. A few days ago, the nurse in the ophthalmologist's office had shaken her head when she read his card. "Zigmund Vla . . . Vla-sik. Tha's a right strange name," she said. Zig said nothing; he read the nameplate on her uniform: "Floralene Booger."

"Yessir, got um right in the cockpit."

"Tha's what happened to the radio."

"Plane would of crashed."

"It did!"

"I mean, im-med-iately."

"Wuddn't no lightning got um, it was no oxygen."

"Ever hear of automatic pilot?"

"Ol' Red, he had the world by the tay-yul."

"Just think. If he wuddn't so gewd, I mean to git a better job and all, he might not be dead."

They were excited. Not happy, certainly not that.

"Ours is not to reason why . . ." misquoted one, tipping the neck of his bottle into his glass—foam. Zig silently finished the cliché: *Theirs is but to do or die.*

"He didn't feel a thing. No oxygen is just like gettin' drunk. You git happy, laugh, and bingo, out."

Out. It was out of step with how he felt and with the picture that made the feeling. The engines droned. The green instruments glowed. A red light flashed intermittently. A voice came in cuts and scratches over the radio. One of the engines sputtered, quit. A jet fighter cut the flight path and waggled its wings; a brief moon flamed on its fuselage. The cloud horizon tilted sharply, the frame shuddered and came alive, the engine whined, the moon began to spin. Out.

When he left the bar there was a light rain—what he remembered the British calling "bird sweat." He drove past the brave little shacks that fringed the tobacco fields and stood on blocks, stilted oil tanks fast at their unpainted sides. Christ. He tried to give his feeling

for this business a name, but none would come. He told himself that
there were things more deserving of his thought, but he couldn't pull
himself out of the mood. A gothic little riverside cemetery rolled by
on the left. God, how could he ever be buried here? But where else?
Next to his parents up in Rhode Island? He no longer had any
attachment to place. The fondness he had for his hometown was
really a fondness for an old self that vanished a long time ago and
left little residue.

When he swung up the drive past the big magnolia, he saw Odette
haunting the window. He parked the car. The newspaper lay on the
doormat: COACH MISSING AFTER MYSTERIOUS CRASH.

She wore a poutish look. "Alors?"

"Oh hell, I'm sorry."

"I'm waiting here since a half hour. You forget our invitation?"

He looked at her. She was wearing the long blue Persian dress
with the deep square neckline, the one she wore when her parents
last came from Dijon to visit. Lightly made up, no threads of gray,
she still looked very young, pretty—it stung him that he sometimes
forgot. "Yes. No, no, I didn't. Give me a few minutes to clean up."

"Behind your ears," she joked. "At six o'clock we are supposed
to be there."

In the bathroom, Zig shook out the newspaper and read, an awful
feast of details: " . . . pilot of one of the F4s which was following
the plane on its bizarre flight reported he saw it dive 41,000 feet
straight into the dark water off the Virginia coast about midnight.
He said an oil slick formed on the water . . . he had made a pass by
the plane rocking his wings in standard intercept fashion but received no response. There seemed to be no physical damage to the
plane. Running lights were on but the plane was flying with a
darkened cockpit . . . may never know why it mysteriously
wandered 1,000 miles off course and crashed." Then Zig stopped at
a bit of information that was even more freezing: "The plane, a
twin-engine Cessna Conquest, was owned by Medley Construction
Company."

Cessna Conquest. It was the same kind of plane that Channel 8
owned, the one that would fly Zig to Atlanta next week.

The room clinked with the sound of silverware on china. Zig tried to follow the conversation as it flew from face to face: from Vic and Lynda to the boys, Phil and Jeff, at the other end of the table. The Cessna Conquest droned out of the clouds into a canyon-land of white-silver fluff. Phil was being loud. Zig looked at him, a heavy face with red achy skin, and wondered what he had said, why his father, shifting conversation, rolled his eyes and said, "Mr. College Bigshot over there." Vic leaned toward Zig. "So, tell us, what's new at Channel 8?"

Zig came back. "Nothing much."

"That Garden Center ad was a gas. Really. Dressed up like Mother Nature!"

Lynda said, "That what's-his-name is crazy."

Jeff cackled. He had reddish hair, high cheek bones, delicate features. "Maybe he just likes getting into drag."

Odette laughed, a stiff *har har* that told Zig she was still not relaxed with these people they had known for a year now. "Zig, he tells them it is silly but they don't care."

Vic looked at Zig. "So it must get on your nerves."

Vic squinting tipsily through clouds of his own cigarette smoke with small puffy eyes—that's what got on Zig's nerves at the moment. That and the boy's private jokes. And Lynda with the borrowed manner of a TV housewife. "Get on my nerves? Not as much as press deadlines did."

"You like it better?"

"I like not getting an ulcer. And I liked being with Odette and Chris before Chris went off to college. You know?"

"We sure do," said Lynda, making a wristy gesture. "We felt just ter-rible when Phil went off." She smiled with motherly affection at Phil, who began to hum and play an imaginary violin.

Everyone laughed.

"And Jeff's going away next year!"

"Aww, Ma!"

Phil patted his brother on the head. "Poor wittle Jeff."

"Stop it, you'll know how I feel someday."

"Not men. Men do not feel the same."

Zig said, "It's true. We hide in our work. That's why Odette opened the dress shop."

Lynda laughed. "Odette, in two years"—she looked fondly at Jeff who was licking the cake knife—"I'll *need* a job. Keep me in mind."

"Of course. Women must stick together."

Stick together. Zig looked at Vic, a cost accountant, a member of the same swim club, and wondered what, if anything, bonded their families: Yankees living in the South, sons on the edge of the nest, an occasional round of golf. Not much else. But Zig wanted more. He waited for a pause. "What did you think of Coach Ryan?"

"Made the big team in the sky," cracked Phil.

Only Jeff laughed, a thin giggle.

"Not funny," said Vic.

"Phil!" Lynda glared, then slowly turned toward Zig. "Terrible," she said, "Just terrible."

"Bizarre," said Vic.

"Very strange."

"I feel sorry for his wife and children," said Odette.

"It only makes sense," said Phil, slouching back in his chair.

"What do you mean?"

"A dead man doesn't need sympathy, he's beyond feeling."

Vic shook his head. "Still."

Lynda said, "I've heard his wife never saw him that much. He was always at practice or recruiting or on the road or something." Zig wondered what she really meant. Her dark hair, threaded with gray, set off the eyes: a green that glinted, then dulled. But her expression was blank, unreadable.

"I wonder if they were dead," asked Jeff, "when the plane hit the water."

Phil sighed. "Sure they were. They got it when they went above the storm."

Jeff said, "How do you know it wasn't lightning *in* the storm?"

"Because the auto pilot was set *after* the climb. It doesn't set itself, dingbat."

Lynda chanted, "Phil-up!"

Annoyed, Zig asked, "If the plane was on auto pilot, why did it keep climbing?"

"Easy." Phil smirked. "He must have gone to auto, trimmed up, and as the gas went, the plane got lighter and climbed."

"Touché." Zig looked at Lynda and said with a laugh, "He's got all the answers."

"Don't I know it," she said, sweeping the hair from her eyes.

"The Answer Man," said Vic.

Zig didn't feel like laughing with the others. The family had a trace of Chicago in their speech that he found irritating at the moment.

"Just ask me," said Phil, basking. "Cabin leak, no oxygen, they snuffed it."

Snuffed it. A charming TV phrase. Zig watched Vic say, "Odette, more wine?"

"Please."

Zig caught her eye. She got sad and nostalgic after three glasses—it was almost automatic. She smiled and gave him a wink.

"It is getting depressing, no?" she said, as if reading his mind.

"Agree," said Vic, cigarette in one hand, wine glass in the other. "Zig, do your imitation of Duncan."

Lynda laughed. "What a character! Have you seen him lately?"

"This afternoon, in fact. He was on his way for a little pick-me-up."

"I hear he's always picking himself up." She spoke into her wine glass.

"That reminds me," said Vic. "What's the definition of an Irishman?"

Phil and Jeff swapped stoic looks. "We give up, Dad."

"A man who will climb over the bodies of a dozen naked women to get to a glass of beer!"

"Here, Dad, you deserve more wine for *that gem.*"

Phil said, "What's the definition of a football player?"

"We give up," said Jeff sarcastically.

"Somebody who doesn't know the meaning of the word fear . . . or the meaning of many other words!"

Jeff tittered. "I'd say that went for most coaches too."

Phil and Jeff looked at each other and laughed again. There was hostility in the room; Zig could feel it, almost smell it, acrid as dope smoke. Maybe the boys had been smoking. Lynda crimped her mouth in resignation, shook her head, and said to Zig, "He gets a little hyper about jocks. A drunken football player broke his roommate's jaw. For no apparent reason."

"Ma, I haven't got anything against jocks. Coaches either. I just can't stand the mentality that buys a newspaper and throws away everything but the sports page. No joke, I've seen it."

Vic, not listening, said thickly, "But lemme ask you this, Mr. Bigshot. Why do you think those F4s were following the coach's plane?"

Zig stared at the blood gravy on his plate. He didn't like to admit it, but the kid was bright, probably brighter than his parents. And young and strong. Suddenly Zig felt old.

Phil said, "Actually, they couldn't really follow. If they slowed to what that Cessna was flying, they'd almost stall. Know what they touch down at?"

"Hold it, cowboy, I'm asking the questions."

"165 nautical miles per hour. And fly at better than Mach 2."

Zig watched Phil's face warm with satisfaction. Why was the possession of that information so sweet?

Vic said, "I think those F4s were there in case that Cessna started to go down in a populated area." His eyes were threaded with blood.

Jeff said, "What do you mean?"

"I mean"—he puffed on his cigarette to heighten the effect—"they would have smoked it."

"It would have still hit houses."

Vic shook his head, puffed again, and said, "Confetti."

Smoked it. Confetti. God Almighty. Zig took a big swallow of wine and half-listened to Vic recite facts about F4s, their Sparrow missiles. Then Phil introduced a more impressive plane, the Harrier, and began to comment on its features from vertical take-off to rate of climb, how many Gs it pulled in a dive. All this specialized information left Zig dazed, puzzled. What did it have to do with anything? It was like baseball fans testing each other's memory of dusty trivia. Maybe it had something to do with power and expertise, the way Vic drove the TR3 on the back roads to the golf course, downshifting hard on the curves, his CB full of chatter, full of cat-and-mouse involving police radar and allowing for dream footage of bandits at one o'clock high. Zig stared at a silver spoon, at the room in its convex warp, at his own hydrocephalic head. Sound Heaven CBs. Zig helped Duncan work out a one-minute spot: Trouble on the Highway; Saved with a CB. Complete with lightning that briefly tinseled the slanted rain. God. Now they were all talking about close calls they had had or knew about. And even Odette was in on it.

"Zig, remember that flight from Washington?"

He did.

"A John Wayne pilot like in, ah. . . ."

"The High and the Mighty."

"Yes, yes!"

As Odette spoke, Zig remembered the details: a bouncy, erratic flight, the pilot weaving the aircraft to avoid a storm, then bringing them down through an absolutely minimal ceiling. The clouds suddenly snapped away, and the ground and trees were there beside the concrete runway, pricelessly green, all the passengers cheering. Fright stories. Zig was tempted to join in, say something, perhaps, about his Conquest flight next week. Or: *When I was in Vietnam,* he might begin, feeling the power of the phrase, then tell about taking fire at lift-off out of Tan Son Nhut, about the hippy freelancer, his seatmate, who looked at the flames stretching back from the jet pod and laughed wildly, saying, *Well, podner, this may be all she wrote!* Zig was tempted to tell it, but there had already been too much telling, too much idle laughter. And he wanted to keep faith with a deeper feeling. Levity seemed wrong somehow; maybe it wasn't. The freelancer wasn't supposed to laugh, but he did. Zig looked across the table into the living room. The wing chair yawned. The carpets looked suddenly faded; they were tufted with dog hair. Paint was blistered on the baseboard. The dining room windows were black wet squares. Odette described the plane banking sharply. Zig could still see a scribble of lightning. The plane shook violently once. A red light flashed on the panel. Deep canyons of billow silvered below. A fighter shot across the flight path and waggled its stubby chevron wings. A voice crackled on the radio. The starboard engine quit, and the plane began to bank sharply, to turn like Odette's demonstrating hand. "It was frightening."

Frightening. Like the ride home, rain beating on the windshield so hard the wipers couldn't keep up; frightening like strangers who passed for friends, speech that amounted to silence. Wipers clicked. The road was slick, barely visible. God. It could have been the commercial he had made for Duncan. Poetic justice. He thought about the Cessna Conquest and his flight next week. That was frightening, too, and somehow quickening. Odette touched his thigh and leaned against his shoulder. Too much wine. She would probably slip into her more homey French and talk about old friends from the Paris days when she was a secretary and he was in the bureau at the *Herald-Tribune*. Jacques, Michel, Monique. It was the summer they met.
  "T' es fâché?"
  Zig smiled to himself. "Angry? Why should I be?"
  She shrugged. "You were making a puss as I was telling the story of the pilot."
  "I may have frowned, but I wasn't angry."
  "You won't speak French to me?" Her tone was mock angry.
  "I'm too tired. I frowned, I suppose, because I couldn't stop thinking about Coach Ryan. And I didn't like what was going on at the table."
  A huge puddle pounded the underside of the car. " 'Faut faire attention."
  The rain relented a bit. Odette snuggled and pressed her head to his shoulder, pressing to life some old moments: cafés, quais, emerald leafage in the Bois de Boulogne. She said, "You know what one can do this summer?"
  "Tell me."
  She told him.

And, at home in bed, the TV's sedative flicker on the walls, she was telling him again the reasons they should go to Europe, first to Dijon. He had a month coming that summer, or spring, whenever he wanted to take it. It might be the last time to see her parents. "They are no longer young, you know? One never knows."

"I know."

"And Chris, he is doing French at school. He would be able to speak with my parents a bit. That would do him good, you know?"

True. The language and travel experience would be good for the boy, but Zig didn't want to think about traveling, about the awkwardness of being with her parents. His French was rusty, the search for words painful. And everywhere they went, history-hungry tourists would be sniffing about with tourbooks or guides, stuffing themselves with food or information that would never help on a night like this. *165 nautical miles per hour . . . fly at better than Mach 2.*

"Alors, qu'est-ce ' tu pense?"

"Fine. I think it's fine."

In a while she was asleep. Zig stared at a talk show until there was a station break, and the screen held Duncan's face: "A fine stereo *is* affordable. . . . But hurry, time's running out." Zig squeezed the remote selector, and the picture changed to a preacher with burning eyes: " 'And he said unto me, Son of man, can these bones live?' " *Ezekiel,* chapter thirty-seven, verse three. Now I ask *you,* brother ―― " Zig snapped off the set.

He got out of bed and found his slippers and bathrobe. The house was quiet; the world outside was calm. At the hall window, he could see there were traveling clouds, low, inky, and breakthroughs of moon so that the clouds brightened and dimmed like lungs inflating with light. Curious that a strong wind was pushing the clouds while the yard was perfectly still. He looked into Chris's room, at his Ann Margaret poster and beer can collection. He was thirsty and went to the kitchen for juice. It felt good to be walking from room to moonlit room in such a deep quiet. He heard the drone of a light plane and went to the window. The trees stood up like inverted brooms in a brief agitation of wind, which made them appear to be trying to sweep the clouds away. He craned his neck but was unable to catch a glimpse of the red running lights. It was up there though, a fading sound, somebody hunched over a glowing green panel of instruments, peering into the dark for that magic blue runway home. The sky was almost open now. That guy would be luckier than the coach. It was strange. He knew his feeling exceeded the subject. Still. The picture was potent: a tiny plane in a huge expanse of platinum clouds, the cold blue eye of the moon. Something wanted to fly out of him, break through the wall of his body. The yard and trees burned like a phosphor in the moon's light, burned his fingers against the cold glass of the pane.

"Bizarre. Strange. Mysterious. Frightening."

Nothing. They failed, they failed. He stood listening, looking at the silver silence, watching the yard break into eloquence of another order.